FOAL

A Note About
Chinese Cinderella

Adeline Yen Mah's family considered her bad luck because her mother died giving birth to her. They made her feel unwanted all her life. After the death of her stepmother in 1990, Adeline felt compelled to give up her career as a physician to write her life story. Her adult memoir, *Falling Leaves*, was published in 1997 and became an international bestseller. Then, in 1998, Adeline wrote an autobiography for children in response to the many letters she received from young people who also felt unloved and unwanted. The result, *Chinese Cinderella*, is the true story of Adeline's childhood, and has become a much-loved book for young people all over the world.

The book you are holding now, *Along the River*, was inspired by the many imaginative stories Adeline created when she was young and found solace in writing about empowered young women. *Chinese Cinderella* is her own story; *Along the River* relates the adventures Adeline created for CC.

ALSO BY ADELINE YEN MAH

FOR YOUNG ADULTS
Chinese Cinderella
Chinese Cinderella and the Secret Dragon Society
China: Land of Dragons and Emperors

FOR ADULTS
Falling Leaves
A Thousand Pieces of Gold
Watching the Tree

ALONG
the RIVER

A Chinese Cinderella Novel

ADELINE YEN MAH

DELACORTE PRESS

Copyright © 2009 by Adeline Yen Mah
Photographs copyright © 2009 by The Palace Museum, Beijing, China, reproduced by permission of The Palace Museum, Beijing

Visit us on the Web! www.randomhouse.com/teens
Educators and librarians, for a variety of teaching tools, visit us at www.randomhouse.com/teachers

Library of Congress Cataloging-in-Publication Data
Mah, Adeline Yen.
Along the river : a Chinese Cinderella novel / Adeline Yen Mah. — 1st American ed.
p. cm.
Summary: CC suffers a bad fall and, in order to treat her injuries, she undergoes hypnotherapy that reveals her connection to an eleventh-century girl named Mei Lan, who defied convention to befriend a household servant who was a brilliant artist.
ISBN 978-0-385-73895-8 (hardcover trade) — ISBN 978-0-385-90759-0 (hardcover glb) — ISBN 978-0-375-89669-9 (e-book) 1. China—History—Song dynasty, 960–1279—Juvenile fiction. [1. China—History—Song dynasty, 960–1279—Fiction. 2. Reincarnation—Fiction. 3. Hypnotism—Fiction.] I. Title. PZ7.M27633Al 2010   [Fic]—dc22   2009042980

The text of this book is set in 12-point MT Baskerville.

Printed in the United States of America
10 9 8 7 6 5 4 3 2
First American Edition

For my husband, Bob,
and many thanks to my Australian publisher,
Erica Wagner

Contents

ALONG the RIVER

Woman in Black

CC first noticed the woman in black when she stopped at the spice booth to buy salt and soya sauce. The market was packed with people. They crowded the narrow aisles between the stalls, jostling each other and bargaining for the best value. Children raced around, playing hide-and-seek along the cramped passageways, while stallholders called out to passersby, waving their merchandise in the air and shouting out prices.

In all the noise and bustle, CC couldn't be sure how long the woman had been watching her. As soon as their boat had docked in the river town of Feng Jie 奉節, Wu Nai Nai 吳奶奶 (Grandma Wu) had sent her and David on shore to pick up essential supplies. They had been told that Feng Jie was "safe," but it was impossible to be sure in these dangerous times.

"Look out for one another but try not to appear as if you're together," Grandma Wu had said as she handed each of them a straw basket and some money. "Don't talk to anyone unless you have to, and of course don't breathe a word about the American pilots hidden on our boat. Even though Feng Jie is ruled by our President Chiang Kai-shek, Japanese secret agents and collaborators lurk everywhere and we're in constant danger until we get the airmen to Chungking. Their safety depends on your silence."

CC paid for her purchases and packed them into the basket at her feet. As she straightened up she saw the woman in black staring intently at her. Quickly, CC moved away, but she couldn't resist glancing back. The woman was following her, heading in the same direction. She quickened her steps and turned the corner. The woman also turned but maintained a certain distance. Now CC had no doubt: the woman was after her, for sure. But why?

She looked around for David, but he was nowhere to be seen. Her heart quickened and she felt the first trickle of panic. Trying to behave naturally, she continued to buy the foods on Grandma Wu's list: eggs, vegetables, sesame oil, tofu, sugar, rice, flour and fresh fruits. She glanced nervously over her shoulder, hoping against hope that the woman would be gone. But no! There she was, peering furtively from behind a stack of dried cabbage, as if not quite certain that CC was the one she was looking for. But almost sure . . .

Should she make a run for it? No—better behave calmly. Was this woman a Japanese spy? Surely not. She looked so kind, almost motherly. But maybe that was only a disguise. What if she approached CC and started a conversation?

Then perhaps suddenly—WHAM! A hand around the arm. Come with me! Japanese secret police! CC shuddered.

The woman did not look Japanese, but she could be a Chinese collaborator. Did she know about the American pilots hidden on the boat, only a few hundred feet away? Grandma Wu and Master Wu had listened for news on the radio every day since they had rescued the Americans, but they had heard nothing. So they assumed that nobody was searching for them.

"Keep calm, CC. Behave normally," she muttered to herself. But the woman was inching slowly toward her. Their eyes met briefly. CC immediately looked away. She felt her heart racing and a cold sweat running down her back. How scary! What *did* the woman want? CC braced herself.

All at once the woman was right in front of her, blocking the way! CC stared, paralyzed with fear. Would she arrest her? How many years in jail for helping American pilots to escape from the Japanese?

"Excuse me. Are you the niece of Ye Jia Ming 葉家明?"

So the woman had recognized her. But how? There must be millions of twelve-year-old girls in China who looked like her. But the woman had said Ye Jia Ming, which was Big Aunt's maiden name before her disastrous arranged marriage. What else did this woman know? Would CC be taken away and tortured for information about the airmen? She parted her lips to speak, but no words came. Her mouth was dry. She had only one desperate, agonizing thought: she must say *nothing*, because, back on that boat, the Americans' lives depended on her silence! She needed to get away from this woman as fast as possible.

She threw her basket of groceries at the woman, and ran—brushing past a meat-vendor's stall and knocking over a vegetable stand. "Stop her!" the angry merchants yelled, but CC was too quick for them. She had no idea where she was going. She only knew she had to escape— fast! The sound of her feet mingled with the pounding of blood in her ears, blocking everything but fear. Suddenly she was hurtling down steep stone steps toward the pier, taking them two at a time. But, halfway down, she was blocked by a group of workmen carrying large boxes balanced on shoulder-poles. The woman in black would surely catch her now.

It had started to rain and the light was fading. People were yelling and pushing behind her. She needed to get away, but how? Bodies in front, terror behind.

Beside her was a drainpipe leading up to the roof of a building. Out of desperation, CC grabbed onto it and clambered to the top. She had a momentary sense of exhilaration as she looked down at her pursuers. Without kung fu training, they would never be able to catch her. Then, just as she felt as if she might actually get away, her feet slipped on the wet roof shingles and her body plunged into the void. . . .

Coma

David cried out in horror as CC fell from the rooftop, landing with a sickening thud on the dirt below. He had been watching from behind a fishmonger's cart and had seen CC's encounter with the woman in black.

A crowd of people immediately gathered around CC's inert body, including two policemen in uniform. The woman in black was saying something to them. David edged his way closer. He had no idea what to do. Could CC possibly survive such a fall? Then his heart leapt when he saw her chest moving up and down. Although her eyes remained closed, she was breathing and therefore must still be alive!

"I have no idea why she ran away from me," the woman was saying. "I thought I recognized her from a photo. I just wanted to ask for news of her aunt. Nothing else."

"These are troubled times," one of the policeman said. "The girl might have been afraid of something or somebody. Who knows?"

"Thank goodness we're safe here in Feng Jie!" someone in the crowd said.

"Still, there are many pro-Japanese collaborators," the policeman said. "One cannot be too careful. Does anyone know this little girl?"

David stepped forward. "Her name is CC," he said. "She's my friend." To his embarrassment, he started to cry.

The woman in black said sympathetically, "She should be seen by a doctor as soon as possible. I know the Medical Director of the missionary hospital here. He's an American—Dr. Richard Allen. You need to take your friend there in a rickshaw. I'll write a note and tell him what happened. By the way, is your friend the niece of Ye Jia Ming?"

"I have no idea," David said guardedly.

"Ye Jia Ming was my classmate at middle school, and a close friend. I stayed with her once in Nan Tian, before the Japanese massacre. She had many photos of her niece throughout her house. Your friend looks just like the girl in those photos. . . . She *is* her niece, isn't she?"

"I already told you I don't know," David replied with a hint of irritation.

"I feel so bad about her falling like that. Here's the note for the hospital, and this is my card with my name and telephone number. Phone me and let me know how she is. I'm sorry I can't accompany you to the hospital, but I'm late for work. Do you have money to pay the rickshaw driver?"

"Yes," David said. "Please tell him the address of the hospital." He looked at the card and saw that the woman's name was Jiang Fei Fei 蔣 蜚 蜚.

The rickshaw driver seemed to take forever to wend his way through the crowded streets. David kept looking at CC's white, unconscious face, and willed her to wake up. He hadn't realized, until now, how much he always relied on her bravery and sense of humor in dangerous situations. When they got to the hospital, two orderlies and a nurse came running out to help. The woman in black had telephoned in advance and spoken to Dr. Allen.

David handed over the note and was told to wait while CC was taken into the examination room. He sat outside in the waiting room. People kept going in and out, but no one said anything to him. He was about to go down the corridor to look for her when a tall foreigner in a white coat rushed by with a chart in his hand. So he grabbed the man's jacket and asked in a hoarse, anxious voice, "Please tell me what's happening. Is CC going to die?"

The man stopped and looked kindly at David.

"Hello, kid! Are you with the unconscious girl?" he asked in fluent Chinese. "What did you call her—CC? Did you bring CC to us?"

"Yes, I'm David. Her real name is Ye Xian 葉 限, but we all call her CC."

"Well, David, my name is Dr. Allen. Your friend CC has twisted her foot and ruptured some ligaments in her ankle, but it's her head we're more worried about. She's had quite a fall and is still unconscious. We need to admit her to the hospital and keep her under observation until she wakes up. Does she live in Feng Jie?"

"No, but I can get Grandma Wu."

The doctor patted him on the shoulder. "That would be great! By all means, go and get her grandma. Be as quick as you can!" Seeing the anxiety on David's face, Dr. Allen added in a gentler voice: "Try not to worry. People's heads are my specialty. Your friend is in good hands with me."

Hospitalization

As soon as Grandma Wu saw David running alone toward the boat with his dirty, tearstained face, she knew something must have gone terribly wrong. But she wasn't prepared for the dreadful news he brought. Dropping everything, she hurried over to the hospital at once.

After speaking to Dr. Allen, she knew she faced a difficult choice. Should she stay with CC in Feng Jie, or go back to the boat and escort the American airmen to safety? In the end she ordered her son, Master Wu, and the three boys David, Sam and Marat to deliver the Americans to Chungking. She herself left the boat to look after the comatose CC, staying at the guest hostel attached to the missionary hospital and sitting by CC's bed every day.

Jiang Fei Fei, the woman in black, came to the hospital the morning after the accident to check on CC. She worked as a nurse attached to the local Red Cross station and was much saddened to hear that Big Aunt had been killed by the Japanese. Jiang Fei Fei and Grandma Wu soon became friends. Through Fei Fei's contacts, Grandma Wu was able to get the latest news from Chungking.

Although CC had broken no bones, she remained unconscious and required constant monitoring. Day after day, Grandma Wu helped the nurses wash and turn her from side to side as she lay, white-faced and still, on the narrow hospital bed. She wanted to be there when CC woke up, mainly to reassure her but also to stop her from saying anything indiscreet about the American airmen and the rescue mission.

During the first ten days, there were momentary signs that CC was emerging from her coma. Her eyelids would flicker and she would mutter something indistinct. But then she would lapse back into oblivion. From time to time, she called out quite clearly "Ah Zhao 阿趙!" and "Gege 哥哥 (Older Brother)!" but nothing she said made much sense.

Dr. Allen continued to hope that CC would make a full recovery. He instructed Grandma Wu to keep talking to her as if she could hear everything. So Grandma Wu passed the days chatting to CC and reading to her from newspapers and books she found in the hospital library. However, as day after day went by and there was no change, she couldn't help worrying. The only good news was from Jiang Fei Fei, who reported that the Americans had arrived safely in Chungking. A ceremony had been held during which President Chiang Kai-shek himself had awarded the airmen medals for bravery, before flying them home to America. Soon afterward, Grandma Wu heard directly from her son that he and the boys were safe and well looked after by the Nationalist government. They would remain in Chungking until they heard from her.

Then one morning, three weeks after her fall and without any warning, CC regained consciousness. On opening her eyes, she was amazed to find herself in a hospital bed, with Grandma Wu sitting at her bedside reading a newspaper. As nurses gathered in her room and celebrated her awakening, CC noticed that the date printed on the daily paper was July 25, 1942. Remembering the American pilots telling her about Independence Day as the boat approached Feng Jie on July 4, CC realized with a shock of recognition that she had been unconscious for three whole weeks!

At first she could hardly stay awake for longer than an hour at a time. Repeatedly, she had to be reminded of where she was and how she had got there. She complained of a severe headache and often seemed confused. She asked about David, but could remember little about the day of her fall in the market.

Gradually, the periods of wakefulness grew longer, but CC remained muddle-headed and sickly. She was plagued by blinding headaches, and her sleep was disturbed.

Grandma Wu spoke to Dr. Allen about her concerns. "I know she has been very ill, but CC is really behaving most strangely. She often doesn't respond to her own name and she forgets other people's names too. She keeps calling me Nai Ma 奶媽 (Nanny or wet nurse). This morning the nurse woke her up so that she could dress her injured foot, but as soon as she brought the bandages near the bed, CC screamed and cowered away from her as if she were being attacked. It took a long time to convince her that the nurse was not going to hurt her. She also seems very sad about something. From time to time she mutters the name Ah Zhao over and over. I know she has recently lost her Big Aunt, whom she loved very much, but she won't talk about it, and to be honest, I don't think that's the problem."

Over the last few weeks, Dr. Allen and Grandma Wu had developed great respect for one another. She learned that he was the son of missionary parents and had been born in China. After graduating from medical school in America, he had returned to China and founded the hospital in Feng Jie. He, in his turn, was impressed by her intelligence, calmness, emotional stability and quiet strength. He knew she wasn't the kind of person to worry about nothing.

"Perhaps it's time for CC to spread her wings a little," he suggested. "The torn ligaments in her ankle and foot have not yet healed, but with the help of crutches she could take short walks. You might like to show her different parts of the hospital or even the garden. This will help her regain her strength. It might even relieve her headaches and enable her to sleep more soundly."

Although her room was pleasant enough, with its white-painted furniture and windows opening onto the grounds, CC was glad to leave it for a while. She took some time to get used to the crutches, but was soon managing so well that she could go for short walks around the hospital by herself. She came across a stack of magazines and publications, in Chinese and English, on a wooden table in the main entrance hall. Among them was a large, handsomely bound volume called *The History of Art and Literature in China.*

It was a heavy, hardback tome filled with poetry and photos of old paintings. There was something about the book that immediately intrigued CC. She asked Grandma Wu to carry it into the garden, so she could sit on one of the wooden benches under the trees and read it properly.

Together they looked through the photos of different paintings, but there was one in particular that fascinated CC.

"Look at this one! Grandma Wu! Where would I have seen this painting before?"

Grandma Wu put on her glasses to study it closely. "I don't know, CC. This is a very famous painting from the Song Dynasty. It's called *Qing Ming Shang He Tu* 清明上河圖 (*Along the River at Qing Ming*). You may have seen a copy of it, but I doubt you would have seen the original."

Grandma Wu tried to interest CC in the other paintings in the book, but CC kept flipping back to *that* painting, her eyes fixed on the panorama of river traffic and city life depicted more than eight hundred years ago. It seemed familiar somehow—oddly evocative. It bothered her that she couldn't understand why she found it so appealing. She marveled at the artist's skill in rendering hundreds of people, animals, carts, stalls, buildings and boats at a particular moment in time onto a long, narrow picture. How wonderful, she thought, that he should have had the ability and patience to capture a slice of Song Dynasty life and preserve it for eternity.

She read the caption beside the painting and learned

that the name of the artist was Zhang Ze Duan 張 擇 端, a court painter who lived from AD 1085 to 1145. She found his name as haunting and arresting as the picture. It too had a familiar ring, as if it were someone she had known a long time ago. But who was Zhang Ze Duan? Where did he come from? And how had she heard of him? Had someone mentioned his name to her sometime in the past? Or could she have met one of his descendants?

For the next few days, CC was kept busy attending physiotherapy sessions for her foot, eating her meals and exercising in the garden. But whenever she could, she would go back to the book and look at the painting. Each time she held the volume in her hand, strange things would happen. Meandering through her mind, jumbled and unbidden, would tumble sights, sounds, smells, gestures, laughter and snatches of conversation. Sometimes, she even thought she could recall fleeting expressions of people she had encountered long ago. There they were! Familiar and elusive at the same time. Were these memories or hallucinations? She didn't know.

Her headaches and feelings of confusion continued. She tossed and turned through the night. She started taking the big picture book into bed with her and staring at the Song Dynasty painting for hours on end. She found the images of boats, bridges, gateways, hamlets and markets soothing yet stimulating. She felt she had been in that city before; had walked along the riverbank and bought things at the market stalls; had seen all those people, dressed in their robes, strolling and gesturing, flying kites and sailing boats, eating and drinking, gambling with dice and placing bets

14

on cricket fights, laughing and talking. Yet a part of her knew that this peculiar feeling of having been there before was not connected with any real event she could remember. It was like a doubling of consciousness.

She confessed to Grandma Wu that, for reasons she couldn't explain, this particular painting touched a chord in her that resonated with emotion and nostalgia. She found herself drawn deeper and deeper into its aura. As her appetite increased and her body grew stronger, the painting exerted an increasingly dangerous spell. At times, she was almost afraid to look at it for fear that she might be going mad.

Again, Grandma Wu talked to Dr. Allen about her concerns, including CC's obsession with the painting. He too was puzzled by CC's slow recovery. The medical staff had done everything possible, and there were no signs of any undiagnosed physical problem. However, the symptoms of headaches, anxiety, amnesia and insomnia continued. After consultation with Grandma Wu and with CC herself, Dr. Allen decided to treat CC with hypnotherapy.

"I've had a lot of experience in this area, and a great deal of success," he reassured them both. "It's really a very straightforward process, and I think we should start as soon as possible—how does tomorrow sound?"

Hypnotherapy

The next afternoon, Grandma Wu helped CC get dressed in street clothes for the first time since her accident. CC felt strange putting on her blouse and slacks instead of the hospital pajamas that she had worn for so long. Together, they found their way through the corridors to Dr. Allen's office.

Dr. Allen looked up and smiled as they came in. His ground-floor office consisted of a large rectangular room with big windows overlooking the garden. Facing the door was an enormous writing desk surrounded by three chairs. Under the window was a comfortable red leather recliner. On his desk were writing materials and a typewriter, a vase of fresh flowers, a telephone and a sophisticated-looking machine.

"Here's my favorite patient! Welcome to my part of the

hospital for a change, CC. How're you feeling today—still willing to give my idea a go?"

CC swallowed nervously and nodded. Grandma Wu patted her hand and said, "Remember, I'll be right outside the room, CC. There is nothing to be afraid of."

A few minutes later, CC was settled in the red recliner while Dr. Allen pulled out a chair opposite her.

"Now, I don't want you to be frightened," he said. "All I'm going to do is help you feel very relaxed so that you can tell me some of these dreams that have been troubling you. This might relieve your headaches and help you feel less confused. Hopefully, you will then start to sleep better at night. All right?"

"Will I be awake when I'm talking to you?"

"Absolutely. But after our session you might not remember what we've talked about."

"Will you tell me?"

"Yes, of course." Dr. Allen pointed to the gleaming, state-of-the-art machine on his writing desk. "See this wire recorder? This will record our conversation. In time, I will let you listen to the recording so you'll know exactly what you said. Okay now?"

CC thought about it for a moment. To her surprise, she found that she didn't feel quite as nervous as before.

"Yes, I'm fine."

"Good! Now look at this ball dangling in front of your eyes and just concentrate on listening to what I say. Your eyelids are getting heavier and heavier. You are becoming sleepy. Soon, you will start to feel more and more relaxed. . . ."

CC wasn't quite sure she believed him, but she did as she

was told. She stared at the little green ball swinging back and forth before her eyes: right to left, left to right. Her eyelids were indeed getting heavier and heavier. After what seemed like no time at all, she heard Dr. Allen saying, "That's enough for today, CC. You can open your eyes now."

The light from the window had disappeared completely. Outside, it was now pitch black.

"Did I fall asleep?" she asked. "Aren't we going to do the hypnotism?"

Dr. Allen laughed as he helped CC out of the recliner. "It's all over. You did extremely well for a first session. Don't worry! Remember what I said before. It's quite common not to recall much about it."

CC's legs felt strangely heavy and wobbly, not like her own legs at all. She struggled with her crutches and was glad Grandma Wu was there to look after her.

Richard Allen sat for a while after the door closed behind CC. He looked at the wire recorder and shook his head as if he could not quite believe what he had heard. He pressed the return button and listened to his own voice talking to CC.

DR. ALLEN: Now, CC—are you feeling comfortable?
CC: Yes, thank you.
DR. ALLEN: Good. Now I want you to think back to the day when you fell. Can you remember?
CC: Yes.
DR. ALLEN: Okay then. You're running through the market and suddenly you see someone who scares you. You are

running . . . running . . . and all at once you fall. What do you remember now, CC?

(Silence for half a minute.)

CC: Why are you calling me CC? My name is Zhang Mei Lan. Zhang 張 is my surname and Mei Lan 美 蘭 (Beautiful Orchid) my given name.

DR. ALLEN: You have been overheard calling out the names of Ah Zhao and Gege quite frequently. Who are they?

CC/MEI LAN: Gege is my older brother. He and Ah Zhao are best friends. Ah Zhao is the greatest artist in the world. I need to read him the poem I'm writing. It's about a marble snail he carved for me.

DR. ALLEN: Is Ah Zhao a man?

CC/MEI LAN: He's a seventeen-year-old boy.

DR. ALLEN: Tell me about him. Start from the beginning.

CC/MEI LAN (irritably): I'm not here to report on Ah Zhao.

DR. ALLEN: Why are you here, then?

CC/MEI LAN: To pray.

DR. ALLEN: Pray for what?

CC/MEI LAN: Does one always have to pray for something? Prayer is more than just a request for favors. It's a form of communication.

DR. ALLEN: Communication with whom?

CC/MEI LAN: With the dead.

DR. ALLEN: Is Ah Zhao dead?

CC/MEI LAN: I don't know. . . . I mean, yes and no.

DR. ALLEN: Explain yourself.

CC/MEI LAN: The things that Ah Zhao could not say to me when he was alive, he can now tell me, if he is indeed dead.

DR. ALLEN: How can he tell you if he's dead?

CC/MEI LAN: He tells me through my prayers. A prayer is not just a string of words, or the sound of a murmuring voice. Communicating with the dead goes far beyond that.

DR. ALLEN: What *is* a prayer, then?

CC/MEI LAN: A prayer is the meeting of two minds in a moment that goes beyond time. It may never have happened in real life, but it's always happening.

DR. ALLEN: And how old are you, Mei Lan?

CC/MEI LAN: I was born thirteen years ago, on the seventh day of the fifth moon of the Sixth Year of the reign of Emperor Zhezong (AD 1091), the Year of the Goat.

DR. ALLEN: And what can you tell me about where you live, Mei Lan?

CC/MEI LAN: I live with my parents and Gege (Older Brother) in a mansion with a sloping tiled roof in Bian Liang 汴 梁, the capital city of China. Our home has three shaded courtyards as well as a garden full of beautiful rocks and rare plants.

DR. ALLEN: Tell me more about your family.

CC/MEI LAN: My *baba* 爸 爸 (father) used to be Mayor of Dongwu in Shandong Province but is now chief assistant to Commissioner Ye Di 葉 棣. He is a very important and busy man.

Unlike other rich men, Baba has just one wife, my stepmother, whom I call Niang 娘 (Mother). Gege and I are their only children. Our real mother died giving birth to me, and Baba married Niang one year later. Niang is famous for her beauty, but, for as long as I can remember, she has been an invalid suffering from some nameless malady. She spends her time in her room applying makeup to her face, arranging her hair or staring at herself in the glass. Her wardrobe is full of garments made of expensive fabrics, such as silk and imported wool, and her hair is always done in an elaborate style. Some of her hairdos are more than ten *cun* 寸 (about ten inches) tall, adorned with jeweled pins and tiny jade combs. Her bathroom is full of pots of powders and rouges, tweezers to remove eyebrow hairs, fine combs and tiny scissors.

Besides having beautiful eyes, fair skin and an alluring figure, Niang has small bound feet barely three inches long. Baba calls them his perfect golden lotuses. She takes tiny steps and she sways in a really graceful way when she walks. She has more than two hundred pairs of shoes, which she displays on a special shelf in her room. The shoes are made of silk and come in all the colors of the rainbow, with matching cloth soles. Many are embroidered with elaborate pictures of birds, flowers and leaves. She changes her shoes three or four times a day and wears shoes even when she sleeps at night.

Legend has it that swarms of matchmakers approached her parents when Niang was a young girl. At that time, foot-binding was not as popular as it is today, and Niang was one of the very few marriageable young girls who had small feet. The longer my *lao lao* 姥姥 (maternal grandmother) held out, the more unbelievable the offers that came in. Nobody was good enough. It was rumoured that the Crown Prince himself had expressed interest. Unfortunately, he already had a main (big) wife, but he offered to take Niang into his Imperial Palace as one of his little wives or concubines. This Lao Lao refused to allow. But if Niang had married the Crown Prince, Lao Lao could have become the mother-in-law of a future emperor!

"The years rolled by and suddenly Lao Lao realized that Niang was twenty-five. Most girls are married by the time they are fifteen, and although Niang was still beautiful, people had stopped asking to marry her. Then one day, Lao Lao heard rumours that Baba's wife, my birth mother, had suddenly passed away. Besides having no wife, Baba had the added advantage of not having even a single concubine. This was highly unusual for a man in his position but would obviously make life easier for the new woman in Baba's life, whoever she might be. Although Baba was not an Imperial Prince, he came from a good family and was a Han Lin 翰林 scholar. The very next day, Lao Lao summoned the best match-maker in the capital city to arrange the marriage.

According to my *nai ma*, they had a lavish wedding with more than five hundred guests. From the beginning of the marriage, Niang had very little energy and spent most of her time in bed. At first, everyone thought she was pregnant. Months and years went by, but no baby appeared. Gradually, it was accepted that Niang suffers from some sort of mysterious illness that nobody talks about.

Niang and I were both born in the Year of the Goat, two cycles or twenty-four years apart, but she seldom acknowledges my presence when we are in the same room. I'm simply not important to her. Unlike her, I'm not beautiful. Unlike Gege, I'm not a boy. Whenever we are alone, she often says and does cruel things to me. At best, she treats me like part of the furniture. It's been like this for nearly as long as I can remember.

DR. ALLEN: So who looked after you if your *niang* was always ill?

CC/MEI LAN: I was looked after by Nai Ma, who shares my room and has been with me for as long as I can remember. Baba once told me that Nai Ma had been hired by my own mama, before she died. Nai Ma is a peasant woman from the countryside. She has large feet, buck-teeth and a pockmarked face, but she works hard. Niang says she is ugly, but Nai Ma and I love each other. Perhaps it's because I'm not beautiful either—I have a foot that's all twisted and I can't move very gracefully.

Although Nai Ma can hardly read, she was the one who persuaded Baba to include me when Baba hired Teacher Lai to be Gege's private tutor. It was because of Nai Ma that I learned to read and write from an early age.

When I was five years old, Teacher Lai gave Gege and me a separate notebook each, together with a little brush. He told us to make drawings of our daily life and write a verse or story to describe them. Since Gege prefers to draw, while I like to write, his book is full of images, whereas mine is full of words.

DR. ALLEN: So you like to write . . . but you also like looking at paintings, don't you, Mei Lan? Tell me about the painting of *Along the River at Qing Ming*. Why is that painting so special?

CC/MEI LAN (becoming agitated): No, no! Don't ask me about the painting. It's our secret. Only Ah Zhao knows about the painting . . . and Gege . . . Gege, please don't say anything. You promised not to tell anyone! They'll stop us. I need to go. . . . I need to run, but I can't. . . . The market is so crowded I can't get away. Where's David? I need to get back to Grandma Wu.

DR. ALLEN: Calm down, CC. We won't remember anything you don't want to. Just relax and let your mind go blank again. I want you to stop remembering for a while. . . .

The voices on the recorder stopped, but the machine kept whirring while Richard Allen sat lost in thought. Finally, he fed some paper into the typewriter on his desk and began to type.

Case History of CC by Dr. Richard Allen, MD.

CC (Chinese name: Ye Xian 葉限) is a twelve-year-old Chinese girl who suffered severe head injury after a fall from a height of thirty feet. After regaining consciousness, she developed symptoms of headaches, insomnia and anxiety as well as feelings of déjà vu and amnesia. She had difficulty recalling her name, family history and recent events, but identified strongly with a famous painting of the Northern Song Dynasty titled *Along the River at Qing Ming*. In an attempt to relieve CC's neurological symptoms, I began to administer hypnotherapy treatments. During her first hour under hypnosis, CC claimed to be a young girl named Zhang Mei Lan, living during the Song Dynasty.

I recorded and transcribed CC's words under

hypnosis, and will continue to do so. At the conclusion of her treatments, I will allow CC to hear Zhang Mei Lan's story in the hope that it will give her insight into her condition, rid her of her headaches and enable her to make a total and complete recovery.

A Real Awakening

After this first hypnotherapy session, CC slept like a baby right through the night. Even better, the next day she was free from headaches for the first time since awakening from her coma.

Grandma Wu began to hope that all might be well. "Perhaps now she might start to recover and be her old self again," she said to Dr. Allen.

"It's certainly a good beginning," Dr. Allen said. "But I think you should listen to this, Madame Wu." And he played her the recording of CC talking as Mei Lan.

Grandma Wu sat and listened in silence. "I don't understand. Has the fall damaged her brain in some way? Does she really think she is this girl Mei Lan? How does she know so much about the customs of the time?"

Dr. Allen shrugged his shoulders. "We understand so little

about the workings of the mind. CC may have damaged a part of her brain called the temporal lobe during her fall. She could also be imagining all this, remembering things she has read or heard in the past."

Grandma Wu thought for a while. "Of course, it's also possible that CC is genuinely recalling events from a previous life. The fall might somehow have caused her to experience a real awakening and remember a past life in a way that most people cannot."

Dr. Allen smiled. "You know that reincarnation is not believed by most Westerners."

Grandma Wu nodded. "Just because people don't believe in something doesn't mean it isn't true."

Dr. Allen glanced at his notes. "I think we need to find the cause of CC's obsession with that Song Dynasty painting and what she—or at least Mei Lan—is running away from. I can't help feeling that the answers to her illness lie within that particular painting. I would like, with your permission, Madame Wu, to keep CC here and continue treating her with hypnotherapy until she recovers completely."

Grandma Wu agreed. "The treatment you gave her yesterday certainly helped her sleep. Besides, CC is not fit enough to travel yet. I believe you have her best interests at heart, Dr. Allen, so we are in your hands."

For the next two weeks, CC stayed at the hospital and continued her sessions with Dr. Allen. Each day she grew a little stronger and happier. Although the dreams troubled her less and less, she continued to be drawn to the Qing Ming painting. She spent hours tracing the outlines of the figures in the picture—as if they could tell her what she needed to know.

Besides administering hypnotherapy day after day, Dr. Allen worked long into the night researching the medical literature, reading pertinent articles and writing his reports. Grandma Wu, meanwhile, stayed constantly at CC's side. She was always ready to read to CC, accompany her on walks, and play a game of *wei qi* 圍棋 (go) or chess. Finally, the day came when Dr. Allen invited CC and Grandma Wu into his office to hear his conclusions.

He began by telling CC that what she was going to hear might surprise her, but that she wasn't to worry in any way. She was fully recovered from her fall and, by listening to the recording, she would begin to understand many of the things that had been troubling her for the last few weeks.

"Okay if we begin, CC?" he asked.

"Yes—of course," she replied. "I can't wait."

Dr. Allen played the recording from their very first session together. CC listened intently while Grandma Wu watched her anxiously.

When the machine stopped playing, Dr. Allen switched it off and waited as CC struggled to make sense of what she had just heard.

"But what does it all mean . . . who is Mei Lan? Did I tell you any more about her?"

"Actually, this was just the very beginning, CC. It took a few sessions to come out, but Mei Lan's story really began when her father brought home a young orphan boy to be a companion and servant to Mei Lan's older brother. I have the whole story here in Mei Lan's own words, and I think we should hear it from her. It will be easier for me to explain why you know so much about that painting when you hear the whole story."

Grandma Wu held up her hand. "If we're going to be listening to several hours of recording, may I suggest that we make CC as comfortable and relaxed as possible while listening?"

"Certainly, I will have my secretary bring in some tea. Meanwhile, please make yourself comfortable as well, Madame Wu. I suggest that CC lie on the red recliner—which is where she told me Mei Lan's story—while you and I remain in our chairs."

CC lay down quietly on the recliner, deep in thought, while the tea was being prepared. At last she was going to hear the whole story about that mysterious painting. Had she seen it somewhere before? Why did it look so familiar? Would the pieces of the puzzle finally fit together so she could stop worrying?

When everything was ready, the small group made a circle round the wire recorder to hear Mei Lan's story.

Barbarian Orphan Boy

Our house has always been full of beautiful things. Besides being a high government magistrate, our father, Baba, is also a famous art connoisseur, with a collection of bronzes, jades, porcelains and paintings unequaled anywhere except in the Imperial Palace. It's his love of art that led directly to Ah Li's 阿 李 joining our household. Three years ago, when I was ten years old, Baba came across Ah Li in a jade shop on the main thoroughfare. He watched, mesmerized, as Ah Li worked on a pair of matching earrings he was carving out of a tiny piece of jade. When Baba learned that Ah Li was an orphan, toiling without wages, he pitied him and took him home to work for our family and be a companion to my brother Gege.

I can still remember the day Ah Li arrived. Baba was so

excited that he sent for us as soon as he got home, to tell us about Ah Li's amazing skill.

"I've never seen such talent. This boy has had no training at all. Yet he shows such wonderful understanding, as well as enormous technical ability. He's the best jade carver I've ever encountered."

I remember looking at Ah Li and thinking that he didn't look like anyone I had ever met. Later on, I found out why this was so. Ah Li is not *Han Ren* 漢人 (of Han origin). His ancestors came from a foreign country far away to the west. Ah Li cannot read or write but is able to create anything he fancies out of wood, bamboo, clay, jade or stone. He can also make things grow in the garden. He and Gege spend hours cutting shrubs into the shapes of tigers, monkeys, dogs and birds.

I try to help them sometimes, but Gege always shoos me away. Gege was born in the Year of the Ox, whereas Ah Li was born in the Year of the Rabbit. Although Gege is two years older, Ah Li is half a head taller and already has fine hair growing above his upper lip. He has tousled, dark brown hair, big round eyes and a prominent but crooked nose. Old Ah Wang 阿王, Baba's number-one manservant, calls him *Da Bi Zi* 大鼻子 (Big Nose).

Ah Wang has worked for us since Baba himself was a baby. He's always scolding Ah Li for laziness. Ah Li enjoys gardening but hates cooking, doing laundry and dusting and cleaning.

Like Gege, Ah Wang was also born in the Year of the Ox, four *sheng xiao* 生肖 cycles (forty-eight years) earlier. Like most Ox people, he is strong-willed and stubborn. Ah Wang is a foot shorter than Ah Li, with bow legs and a bald head fringed by wisps of white hair. Something's wrong with his back because he's unable to stand up straight, and he walks with his shoulders hunched and his head bent forward at all times. The boys don't like him, and call him Hunchback.

Ah Li tries to avoid Ah Wang as much as possible. He spends his time tending the flowers and shrubs in the court-yards, walking around with his hands in his pockets and whistling as if he's lord of all under Heaven. Gege often saunters into the garden to "help" Ah Li, instead of doing his homework and studying the Confucian classics.

At times, Ah Wang reports Gege's truancy to Baba. He says Ah Li is a bad influence and will make Gege fail the *Jin Shi* 進 士 (Imperial Examination). Baba usually laughs and says that Gege understands how important the exami-nations are and will not dishonour the Zhang family by failing. He also says that someone who carves jade as well as Ah Li must be intelligent. However, to stop Ah Wang from complaining to Niang, he forbids the boys from play-ing in the garden where Ah Wang can see them. So the two boys begin spending time in Ah Li's garden shed, where he sleeps.

While they are in there, instead of memorizing Confu-cian sayings and composing essays, Gege and Ah Li make amazing objects such as wooden flowers, bamboo cups, paper-cuts, clay figures and stone sculptures. They laugh and joke and have so much fun that I can't resist going there myself.

Under Ah Li's direction, Gege and I have become will-ing helpers in transforming his shed into a playhouse. First we clean out the rubbish and sweep the earthen floor.

Beneath the window, we erect a platform of long, wooden planks and cover it with bamboo matting to transform it into a sort of bed for sleeping, sitting or jumping. Against the wall, we build a large wooden box with a lid, for storage. Finally, we help him make a round table by placing a large slice of polished tree trunk on a flat piece of beveled stone. Outside the hut, we frame the door with two rows of bamboo trunks of equal height and roundness. We put two wooden benches facing the garden with their backs to the bamboo. Throughout the monthlong process, Ah Li directs us like a general, placing a piece of stone here, or removing a shrub there. He emphasizes over and over that *space* and *voids* are as important as flowers and trees in the creation of beauty and harmony.

We spend many happy hours creating our playhouse in the garden, but one day we look up and see Ah Wang's beady little eyes glaring at us through the window.

"Looks like trouble ahead," says Gege. As usual, he's right.

Painting Lessons

Ah Wang tells Niang about us. He says that Gege is wasting time with Ah Li, and that I'm encouraging them. Niang scolds me and gives me her usual lecture—the one where she says: "Isn't it enough that you're rebellious, lazy, ugly and unfilial? Do you have to prevent Gege from studying as well?" Then she gives me a slap (which I was expecting) and follows it with a painful, sly pinch (which I wasn't). The worst bit is that she tells Baba, who gets really cross. As punishment, he orders Gege to spend more time practicing his *shu fa* 書法 (calligraphy) so his handwriting will impress the Imperial Examiners.

The lucky part of the whole business, though, is that Baba doesn't tell us we have to stop spending time with Ah Li. So, the next afternoon, when Ah Li has finished his chores and Gege has recited his Confucian sayings, we meet up.

"It's just not fair," Gege says, kicking the stone support under the table. "I'm sick of practicing my *shu fa*—it's boring. I'd much rather paint pictures of objects I can see."

"It's all Niang's fault," I say. "She hates it if we have any fun at all."

"How does *she* know what you do?" Ah Li asks. "She doesn't leave her rooms often enough to find out, does she?"

"I think she pays Ah Wang to tell her exactly what's going on in the house. A few days ago I saw him speaking to her at her door, and he was jingling coins in his pocket."

Ah Li laughs. "I'm amazed she has to pay Ah Wang— I'm sure he'd gladly tell tales on me for nothing. Anyway, what's so bad about learning *shu fa*? You're lucky to get the chance. I've always wanted to learn how to read and write."

"And you're lucky you don't have to do it!" Gege retorts. "But if you are so keen to learn, then I can teach you. I won't be the best teacher, but I can show you the basics."

Ah Li looks delighted, so I help Gege carry the four "scholars' treasures" (*wen fang si bao* 文 房 四 寶—ink-stick, ink-stone, brush and paper) to Ah Li's shed, and place them on the big round table. We show Ah Li how to make fresh ink by grinding the ink-stick in water, against the ink-stone.

Gege moistens his brush with ink, and teaches Ah Li the

correct way of holding the brush vertically between his third and fourth fingers. He begins with a few simple characters such as *xin* 心 (heart), *Tian* 天 (Heaven), *ren* 人 (man) and *li* 力 (strength). To our amazement, from his first stroke, Ah Li's *shu fa* looks far better than Gege's or mine, even though he has never done this before. Unlike my childish squiggles or Gege's impatient scrawls, Ah Li's *da zi* 大字 (big characters) are balanced, harmonious and imbued with emotion. For instance, the three dots and single curved line in Ah Li's word *xin* 心 (heart) appear to have emerged from his very own heart through the power and velocity of his brush.

"How did you *do* that?" Gege asks, impressed.

"Do what?" Ah Li replies.

"Sure you haven't practiced calligraphy before?"

"You must be joking!"

Next morning, Gege shows Ah Li's big characters to our tutor, Teacher Lai.

"Amazing! Full of *qi* 氣 (energy)! Very powerful!" says Teacher Lai. "They remind me of the *shu fa* of the Tang Dynasty master Liu Gong Quan 柳公權 who lived three hundred years ago. I'm curious to see this calligrapher's *cao shu* 草書 (cursive script). Will you ask him to write three or four lines quickly, so I can compare his cursive script with his big characters?"

"He doesn't know how to write cursive script," Gege says. "He's illiterate."

"I don't believe it!" Teacher Lai exclaims, staring at the big characters and shaking his head.

"Maybe he was the famous calligrapher Liu Gong Quan himself in his past life!" Gege jokes.

"I've always considered calligraphy to be a form of art and not a form of literature," Teacher Lai says. "This proves it!"

"Therefore proving that learning Confucian classics by heart is a waste of time!" Gege proclaims.

"Unfortunately, the examiners will be testing your knowledge of Confucian literature, not your *shu fa*. It doesn't do any harm, though, for you to learn to write like this. Tell me, is this man artistic?"

"One of the most artistic people I know!"

"I'd like to see one of his paintings."

"I'll tell him," Gege says, winking at me.

Gege and I begin to learn *shu fa* from Ah Li instead of the other way round. We develop a daily routine. Immediately after breakfast, Gege and I meet Teacher Lai in the study. Being a girl, I only have to learn five new words a day. My lesson is finished in a very short time, but Gege has to spend the entire morning memorizing and interpreting the *Lun Yu* 論語 (*Confucian Analects*), a book of Confucian sayings.

Then Gege needs to write essays and practice his *shu fa*, and of course neither of us can wait to go to Ah Li's shed for the fun to start. We soon progress from calligraphy to drawing the things around us. Ah Li says he's good at *shu fa* because he likes to draw, and *shu fa* is merely another form of drawing.

"Teacher Lai would agree with you," Gege replies. "He

keeps telling me that although calligraphy and drawing are known by different names, they are one and the same."

Gege's drawings have always been far superior to mine. Baba says Gege is quite talented, but he needs to learn to draw what's hidden on the inside as well as what's obvious to everyone.

"I can't draw at all," I tell Ah Li.

"Are you blind?"

"No."

"Can you see?"

"Yes."

"If you can see, then you can draw. Everything you know originates from what you see."

"We're not all artistic like you," Gege says.

"Nonsense! *Xiao Jie* 小姐 (Little Miss) is looking at things without seeing them. What we all need to do is to look at every object with fresh eyes."

"How do we do that?" I ask.

Ah Li suddenly turns himself upside down and stands on his head against the wall.

"Draw me the way I am. Feet up, head down. Imagine you're meeting me for the first time and that's how I like to position myself."

Gege and I laugh, but we obey and draw him upside down. When we finish, Ah Li jumps back to his feet and says, "Phew! I bet you've never stood on your head before. Try it sometime. It's hard work, but I made you see me with fresh eyes just now, didn't I? How did my nose look from that direction?"

"Bigger than ever," Gege shouts, and we laugh again.

"Did you learn anything?" Ah Li asks me.

"Yes—that I prefer to write rather than to draw, but I'd like to be able to do *shu fa* like yours."

"Me too!" Gege says. "Actually, I'd give a lot to be able to do everything the way you do, Ah Li. You're so lucky, Big Nose! I wish I could change my life for yours and have your talents."

"Change your life to that of an orphan slave?" Ah Li looks angry for a moment. "Are you mad? Why would you want a life where you are forever ruled by others?"

Gege bangs his fist on the table. "But that's exactly what my life is like at the moment! You have no idea how bored I am with Confucius 孔子 and Mencius 孟子! I wish those old farts would shut up, because I couldn't care less what they said fifteen hundred years ago. I just want to paint and make things with my hands—like you. The three of us should leave and go and live by ourselves, somewhere else."

"Oh, wouldn't it be wonderful if we could run away together? Go to a distant city far from here and create our own *Tian Xia* 天下 (Land under Heaven)!" I say dreamily, intoxicated by the very thought of it.

"*Shao Ye* 少爺 (Young Master), Little Miss! You must never speak of things like that. Don't even think of it!" Ah Li says in an agitated voice. "If Ah Wang or Nai Ma hear you, they will report me to your *baba* and *niang*. Ah Wang is already complaining that I'm a bad influence."

"Let him complain!" exclaims Gege. "I hate memorizing those ancient books! And you're to stop calling me Young Master, and my sister Little Miss. From now on, you call me *Gege* 哥哥 (Older Brother) and her *Xiao Mei* 小妹 (Little Sister). Do you hear?"

Grasping Ah Li's hand with his right hand and mine

39

with his left, Gege continues, "If we can't make a new life together, at least we can be members of the same family."

Ah Li is clearly very happy, but for once he doesn't know what to say.

Gege smiles. "You see, Ah Li – you aren't the only one who can change the way people look at things. Mind you"—he glances at his latest attempt at calligraphy—"if you can help me change my way of looking at these words, I'll be forever in your debt. Since I can't change places with you, then at least you can teach me to think the way you do."

"I will," Ah Li promises. "Tomorrow, let's hold our brush in our left hand instead of our right. Doing calligraphy with the opposite hand will make us look at words in a new way and give us a fresh, unfamiliar feeling."

It turns out that only Ah Li can do calligraphy with his left hand. Gege and I find it so difficult that we soon give up. But Ah Li's left hand is just as dexterous as his right. In fact, he can draw or write calligraphy with both hands at the same time! Amazing!

Soon, the two of them are spending part of each afternoon painting everything from landscapes to flowers, while I read aloud to entertain them. Baba has instructed Teacher Lai to buy books in the market for us so we can read and expand our minds. Since I love reading, I ask Ah Li to build six bookshelves in his shed, and I fill them with books.

8

Jade Dog

A few months later, Baba summons Ah Li to his study.
"I have a special job for you. Our young Emperor
Huizong 徽 宗 is a gifted artist and calligrapher, interested
in anything to do with art. For His birthday, I want you to
carve Him a dog out of jade. His Majesty was born in the
Year of the Dog, and this is His fifth year on the throne.
Do your best. If His Majesty likes your work, your future
is assured."

"*Lao Ye* 老 爺 (Old Master)," Ah Li replies. "I'm honored. Before I do anything, I need to find a suitable piece
of jade."

"Won't any good piece do?"

"Far from it. Every piece of jade is different. Each has its
own personality. I need to choose one with qualities that
speak to me; preferably a jade with a shape and color that

remind me of something memorable . . . loyalty and constancy, perhaps? Or whatever is at the root of man's love for dogs."

"Well said! Go and find the jade you're looking for and get to work."

Ah Li goes to the city five days in a row and finally finds a greenish white piece of jade that satisfies him.

"It's not only the color," he says to Gege and me as he shows us the stone. "It's the shape and texture as well. Can you see it? In this piece of stone there's a dog that's begging to be released. I'm going to carve His Majesty a jade dog that will defy time, because it will be forever young and full of hope."

Whenever he isn't busy in the garden, Ah Li shuts himself in his shed and works on his jade, behind a screen, permitting no one to see it until it is finished. For the unveiling, he invites only four people: Baba, Niang, Gege and me. He throws back the dust cloth covering the jade and unveils an adorable puppy with floppy ears. Its head is cocked to the right. Its tongue hangs out of its mouth, as if it's panting on a hot summer day. Not only is the dog a work of art, but its very posture suggests carefree youth and happy romps on grassy slopes. All of us are delighted and thrilled. Even Niang is impressed, for once.

"Beautiful!" she exclaims.

"This sculpture will be unique, even in His Majesty's Palace!" Baba says. "It will make your reputation!"

"Congratulations!" I add. "I'm going to write a poem about your jade dog, in my notebook."

Gege is speechless for a long time. Finally, he pats Ah Li

on the back. "I don't know how you did it, but you've released the spirit of a dog from a piece of stone. Remarkable! Simply marvelous!"

Baba presents the sculpture to Emperor Huizong on His birthday. His Majesty is impressed and asks for the name of the artist. Baba reports that Ah Li is an illiterate orphan descended from one of the barbarian tribes to the west of China.

Ah Li thinks this is the end of the matter. But one afternoon, not long after the Emperor's birthday, I'm with Nai Ma in my bedroom. She's going through my clothes chest, checking for anything that might need cleaning, repairing or discarding. This is one of my least favorite jobs—I would much rather be reading or playing a game of chess or *wei qi*—but Nai Ma is being unusually persistent and won't be dissuaded from the task at hand, however tedious it is.

"I have no time to play today, Little Sister. Your *niang* has been complaining that you look unkempt and that you're bringing the family name into disrepute," she says.

"Since when did Niang care what I look like, or even notice that I'm part of this family?"

Nai Ma looks around anxiously, which makes me laugh.

"What—do you think Niang might be creeping up behind you? When did she last set her tiny little feet in my room? I can't remember her being here for five years or more."

"I think you'll find her taking much more interest in you in the future, Little Sister." She picks up my favorite long,

43

faded, blue cloth trousers, which are frayed at the bottom, and puts them in the pile of clothes to be given to the cook's daughter.

"What do you mean, Nai Ma?" I ask as I quickly but quietly move my trousers to the "keep" pile that's going back into the chest.

Nai Ma looks as if she would like to say more, but then she purses her lips and tries to change the subject.

I'm just about to tease her and ask what she was going to say when there's a commotion outside. I race for the stairs as fast as I can, to find out what's happening, and nearly collide with Gege, who has had exactly the same idea.

He takes the stairs two at a time and gets there before me. We look into the courtyard and see nine men, dressed in flowing silk robes, coming through the front gate. Eight of them are carrying an impressive sedan chair draped in yellow silk. Their tall, distinguished leader strides in first and asks for Baba. He's wearing an official hat with the bamboo on each side sticking straight out, signifying his elevated rank. Sitting on the chair is not a person but a large yellow silk envelope.

"These men are from the Palace!" Gege whispers. "Only the Emperor himself is entitled to use a chair draped in yellow silk! Yellow is the imperial color."

We watch as Baba comes forward to greet his visitors. At the sight of the yellow chair and letter, Baba falls to his knees and *kou-tous* 叩頭 (kowtows) nine times. Meanwhile, everyone in the courtyard is kneeling and kowtowing toward the chair, including the visitors.

The leader gets up first and helps Baba to his feet. The two men bow formally to one another.

"General Tong Guan 童貫!" Baba exclaims in an excited voice. "What an honor!"

"I am here to deliver a letter from His Majesty to someone in your household named Ah Li." The leader's voice is surprisingly high and squeaky but full of authority.

Baba turns to Ah Wang, who is kneeling near the wall and trembling with fear. "Go and order Ah Li to come here at once!"

We can see that Ah Wang doesn't want to believe that the letter is for Ah Li, but of course he has to do as he's told.

Ah Li arrives and kneels on the ground in front of the sedan chair. He's ordered to kowtow nine times. The man with the squeaky voice hands Ah Li the yellow silk envelope with both hands, together with five ounces of silver: a special award from the Emperor. Ah Li kowtows again and says that he's unable to read His Majesty's letter because he's illiterate.

"Keep kneeling and listen carefully!" Tong Guan announces haughtily as he unfolds a slip of yellow paper from the envelope. "This is His Majesty's decree: *We are highly pleased with the jade dog that was carved by the barbarian Ah Li. As a mark of special favor, We grant him five ounces of silver. In addition, We give him permission, from now on, to use the name Zhao* 趙—*which is Our royal surname—as his personal surname.*

"Henceforth, your name is no longer Li," Tong Guan announces. "His Majesty has given you the great honor of allowing you to use the imperial surname as your own. From now on, your name is Zhao, the same as His Majesty."

Great excitement follows this announcement. Everyone can tell that Baba is very pleased at such honor being granted to one of the servants in his household. In the midst of the congratulations, I look across at Ah Wang. I think it's safe to say that there's at least one person among us who is not sharing in the celebrations.

Cricket Fight

It doesn't take Ah Wang long to take out his bad temper on the newly named Ah Zhao. He goes out of his way to find the dirtiest and most unpleasant jobs for him to do, such as building a wooden lid for the latrine to hide the filth in the reeking outhouse.

"I don't think I want to be called Ah Zhao," Ah Zhao grumbles to us a few days later. "Ah Zhao has to work one hundred times harder than Ah Li ever did!"

Gege laughs. "Baba says it's a fantastic honor to be granted the royal surname. His Majesty might even commission you to do other work for Him in the future."

"I don't mind what my name is—provided I get paid for my work. Five ounces of silver isn't bad for carving a single jade dog!"

"Not bad? What an understatement!" Gege exclaims. "How does it feel to be a rich man?"

"Much the same as being a poor one. I've entrusted all my money to your *baba*, to keep for me, so I don't lose it or get robbed."

"Speaking of Baba—there's a big birthday coming up for him. It's his fortieth," Gege says. "Now that you're famous, how much will you charge for painting a dragon for his birthday? Baba was born in the Year of the Dragon. He loves dragons, and I know he admires your work. . . ."

"Don't be ridiculous! Your *baba* is my benefactor. I won't charge anything for the painting, but please give me some time. It will be my honor to paint a special dragon for your father's fortieth birthday. But why don't you and Little Sister do something special for him yourselves, as well?"

Gege shrugs. "I don't think so. My work is technically satisfactory, but it's nothing to get excited about, and next to yours it definitely lacks something. Let's face it, Ah Zhao . . . you're the nearest thing I've met to a genius."

Three days later, we walk past Ah Zhao's shed on our way to breakfast and hear crickets chirping. Gege pushes open the door. Inside, we find Ah Zhao tending to an assortment of creepy crawlies, each in its own separate bamboo cage: two crickets, a cockroach, a lizard, an earthworm, a bat, a snake, a frog and a rat. I find his collection repulsive and fascinating at the same time.

"Where do all these nasty animals come from?" I ask.

"Quiet! Genius at work!" Ah Zhao announces. "You're disturbing my new morning routine. I need to take my pets outside for some fresh air."

"Correction! Big Nose is conducting his insect orchestra and training a spooky new menagerie!" Gege says.

I find the bat especially frightening. Its face is a cross between a rat and a fox, but it has wings instead of front legs. Ah Zhao says it hangs upside down when it sleeps.

"Its eyes are so tiny," Gege says.

"Its ears are so enormous," I add.

"And a face only a mother can love," Ah Zhao laughs. "I once saw a bat perch itself on the back of a cow and bury its head in its neck. I thought the bat was drinking the cow's blood, so I poked it with a stick. The bat flew straight at me and scared me out of my wits. It has a wingspan four times the size of its body."

"Why are you keeping all these weird animals in your shed?"

"My goal is to combine the most frightening features of each of my pets here to draw a special dragon for your *baba*'s birthday. My dragon will appear natural and eerie at the same time. Here, take a look at this!"

He shows me a sketch of a horrible monster with horns, antennae, a beard, wings, claws and protruding teeth. The picture sends a shiver down my spine.

Meanwhile, Gege is examining the two crickets, each in its own little bamboo cage covered by wire netting.

"Beautiful, aren't they?" Ah Zhao says proudly. The crickets have black faces with wide jaws, slim reddish brown lacquered bodies and powerful hind legs bent at an angle. One is bigger than the other. Two long antennae protrude from the tops of their heads.

All of a sudden, the smaller cricket raises its wings and begins to sing. The other soon joins in.

"Why don't you put them in the same cage?" I ask.

"They'd kill one another. Crickets need their own space."

"Look at this one!" Gege says. "It has a pretty flower design on its wings. The other one is bigger, but I bet mine is a better fighter."

"No way!" Ah Zhao declares.

"How about a fight between the two?" says a voice from the doorway, and there's Baba with a big smile on his face. Ah Zhao quickly hides the dragon sketch.

"Baba!" Gege cries in delight. "I didn't know you're interested in cricket fights!"

"You don't know much about your old father, do you?" Baba says, striding forward and peering at Ah Zhao's zoo with interest. "Lively specimens! Where do they all come from?"

"I got up at the crack of dawn three mornings in a row to hunt for them in the northern hills," says Ah Zhao. "I spent ages turning over stones, searching under bushes and digging in the undergrowth. It's a special project for your birthday. That's all I'll say for now."

Baba beams with pleasure. "How did you catch the bat?"

"There's this cave where bats like to hang out. Thousands and thousands of them roost together, hanging upside down. I set a trap and caught one. That was easy."

"Which creatures were the most difficult to catch?" Baba asks.

"Believe it or not, the crickets. The season is too early. The few that are around are mostly very small. I tested and rejected a lot of them. Finally, I heard loud chirps coming from beneath a massive stone slab. There must have been dozens of them, because a veritable cricket concert was going on. I dug a couple of holes, took a blade of grass and tried to pry out the insects, but they wouldn't budge. So I poured some water from my drinking flask down the hole. Sure enough, a small cricket sprang out and landed in my net. As soon as I saw it, I knew I was in luck. It was so feisty! While I was examining it, a bigger one crawled out and hopped into the air. I caught it just in time! The two of them are both great fighters! The best!"

"How can you tell?"

"Remember the testers I caught earlier? I pitted them against one another and these two ended up with the best record."

"What do you feed them?" Baba asks.

"I grind up boiled rice, tofu and apple and put the mixture in their cages. I like to hear them sing, so I sleep with them next to my pillow. Their songs bring me good luck."

"How do you know so much about crickets?"

"Cricket fighting is taken very seriously in the village where I was born. Every summer, my *baba* would take me to the northern hills to hunt for crickets. He'd organize cricket fights and place bets on them."

"Did he win lots of money?" Gege asks eagerly.

"Sometimes, but not very often. People cheat a lot."

Ah Zhao turns away, and it's clear he doesn't want to talk about this anymore.

"How does one cheat in a cricket fight?" Baba says.

Ah Zhao is smiling again. "Easy! You paint a scent on your cricket's head, a scent that crickets don't like. Your cricket soon gets used to it, but the other crickets smell it and walk away without fighting."

51

"Fascinating!" Baba says, stroking his beard thoughtfully.

"Baba, why are *you* so interested in crickets all of a sudden?" I ask.

"Little Sister, you are so observant! The truth is, I am obeying orders from my boss, Commissioner Ye."

"Commissioner Ye!" Gege exclaims. "What does *he* want?"

"His niece, Lady An Kai 安愷, is the Emperor's favorite concubine. She has persuaded His Majesty to set up a championship cricket match on her birthday at the Palace. Her Royal Highness wants to win, so she asked my boss to send her a few good fighters. My boss told them it's not cricket season yet, but Lady An Kai doesn't want to wait until autumn."

"My two crickets here will be Lady An Kai's prizefighters!" Ah Zhao avows with confidence.

"Are they male or female?" Gege asks.

"Both are males. Female crickets don't fight."

"Let's have a trial match between them now!" Gege says, rubbing his hands gleefully in anticipation. "My little one against your big one."

"We need to name them first," Ah Zhao says. "Any suggestions?"

"I'll call mine Brave Heart!" Gege shouts.

Ah Zhao turns to me. "Would you like to name the big one?"

"How about Valiant Warrior?" I suggest.

"Valiant Warrior he will be!"

Ah Zhao places the two crickets in a basin. "Old Master!" he says to Baba. "Do you wish to make a bet?"

52

"No money today. But I think Gege's Brave Heart will win."

The two insects are looking at one another, face to face, but there's no interaction. Ah Zhao plucks a bristle from his paintbrush and gently teases the two long feelers protruding from Valiant Warrior's head. Suddenly Valiant Warrior raises his head and opens his fangs. Brave Heart springs into action in response. The two fall on one another violently. They push and pull and wrestle. It's over in an instant.

Sadly, I see Valiant Warrior turn away in retreat while Brave Heart jerks his body, tilts his tail, spreads his wings and begins to chirp a victory song, loudly and triumphantly.

Gege raises his fist in delight, as if he has won the fight himself! "The winner!" he cries. "Brave Heart the Champion!"

"That was merely the first round," Ah Zhao says, smiling. "Didn't I tell you this is a three-round match?"

He removes the two crickets from the basin and places them in a box made of paper. This time, Valiant Warrior refuses to advance no matter how much Ah Zhao pokes him with his bristle. Meanwhile, Brave Heart is marching forward and rattling his feelers aggressively. Seeing this maneuver, Valiant Warrior turns around and retreats to the edge of the box with his feelers pointed downward.

"Valiant Warrior is admitting defeat," Baba says. "He doesn't want to fight anymore. No second round, I'm afraid."

"Don't be so sure," Ah Zhao says. "Watch this!" In one motion, he scoops Valiant Warrior into his hand, makes his hand into a fist and shakes it a few times, then throws the insect into the air with a flourish. Ten seconds later, he catches the flying Valiant Warrior in midair and repeats the routine five times. Finally, he places Valiant Warrior opposite Brave Heart in the paper arena.

This time, things are different. Valiant Warrior faces Brave Heart without flinching, obviously eager for combat. They pause for a second before fencing one another with their feelers. Brave Heart soon spreads his mandibles. Not to be outdone, Valiant Warrior does the same. Their jaws interlock. They push and pull for a few seconds.

Gege and Baba sit on the side of Brave Heart, while Ah Zhao and I are perched behind Valiant Warrior. Ah Zhao hands each of us a blade of beard grass to stimulate the insects. Everyone looks on with trepidation. Gege and Baba cheer loudly at Brave Heart's every move throughout the contest. I say nothing, but can feel my heart racing.

Suddenly Valiant Warrior wrestles Brave Heart to the ground and gets on top of him. Brave Heart retreats into a corner while Valiant Warrior breaks into song.

We can hardly believe our eyes!

"Talk about reversal of fortune!" Gege says dejectedly. "How did you turn Valiant Warrior from loser to winner so fast?"

Ah Zhao shrugs his shoulders. "It's well known that a cricket that loses a match will refuse to fight again until the next day. But I've seen gamblers toss losing crickets into the air and turn them into instant winners by making them fly. I think something happens to crickets when they fly. . . ."

"They start winning!" I exclaim, full of admiration. "You're so smart!"

"What about the third and final round?" Gege says. "To be fair, you must let both of them fly for a little while before they face one another."

"Ah! But life is not fair!" Ah Zhao proclaims.

"You have another trick up your sleeve!" Baba says.

"That's right, Old Master! Watch this!" He twists a tiny piece of paper around the bristle of his paintbrush, walks to the cage that holds the frog and touches the frog gently with the paper.

"What are you doing?" Gege asks.

"Scoop up a cricket in each hand, toss the two crickets in the air and make them fly. Good! Now catch them and hold them in your fists. Which one do you want to win?"

"Brave Heart!" Gege shouts.

"Brave Heart it will be! Is he in your left hand? Good! Release him into the arena and let me apply my magic lotion." He corners Brave Heart and rubs the papered bristle against him.

"What's that for?" I ask.

"Crickets don't like the smell of slime from certain types of frogs. It repels them. Why don't you make Valiant Warrior fly in the air a few more times while Brave Heart gets used to the scent of frog's slime on his own body? Good! Now he's ready. Let's go!"

Ah Zhao places Brave Heart into the basin and signals Gege to release Valiant Warrior. The two crickets face one another. Brave Heart advances aggressively, but Valiant Warrior takes one whiff and turns away, refusing to fight. We're amazed and delighted.

Baba produces a long string of copper coins from his sleeve and turns to Ah Zhao. "Well done! You provided us

55

with a lot of entertainment this morning. Thank you. If you can spare your crickets, I would like to buy them and have you deliver them to Commissioner Ye. Take these coins, go to the market and bring back a couple of gourds for transporting the insects. Keep the change."

He hands me the string of cash to give to Ah Zhao. It's surprisingly heavy. About five hundred round metal coins are strung together with a sturdy piece of red silk, knotted at the end. Each coin has a large square hole in the middle. Surrounding the hole are four inscribed characters, one along each side of the square. "Circulating Treasure of Song," I read. A thought suddenly strikes me.

"These coins are heavy, Baba! What if you buy something really expensive? How would you carry all the coins?"

"You use silver ingots instead of coins," Gege replies. "One thousand coins are the same as one ounce of silver— and there's *fei qian* 飛 錢 (flying money) as well, isn't there, Baba?"

"You're right!" Baba says. "Nowadays we use flying money to buy really expensive items . . . such as houses and land."

I feel confused by the idea of flying money. "Does it have wings and fly away?"

"No wings," Baba laughs. "It's called flying money because it's made of paper, and can be blown away by a puff of wind."

"But paper is cheap!" Gege frowns. "How did paper money become more valuable than copper coins or silver ingots?"

"As Little Sister pointed out just now, long strings of copper coins are too heavy to carry around. So rich merchants started storing their coins at businesses such as pawnshops.

In return, the pawnbroker would give a piece of paper, stating how many coins each merchant had placed with him. When someone needed to withdraw his money, all he had to do was bring his piece of paper to the pawnshop. This practice has been going on since the Tang Dynasty.

"About one hundred years ago, the Emperor ran out of copper coins. So His Majesty began issuing official paper money, printed and guaranteed by the government, instead of coins. Nowadays we use coins to buy small things, and flying money for big purchases."

"Well, I won't need any flying money or silver ingots today," Ah Zhao says. "I can place the crickets in my home-made bamboo cages and deliver them to Commissioner Ye that way."

"Your cages are too flimsy," Baba says. "Gourds are sturdier and more practical for transporting crickets. I don't want those insects to die. Go to the market and bring back two gourds. While you're shopping, I'll write to my boss and tell him about the tricks Lady An Kai can learn to improve her luck with crickets. Transfer your crickets into the gourds when you come back, then deliver the whole lot to the Commissioner at his *yamen* 衙門 (government office)."

"Yes, Old Master!" Ah Zhao says, beaming with pleasure. "In your note, please tell the Commissioner that these two crickets are special. I think they were probably marshals commanding great armies in their past lives. Their souls are filled with fighting spirit and potent *qi* (energy). They will do their owner proud!"

"Enough!" Baba says sternly. "I don't need *you* to tell me what to write. On your way!"

"I'm going with Ah Zhao to choose the gourds!" Gege says. He turns to Baba. "May we go on horseback, to save time?"

"I want to go too!" I say, reluctant to be left behind. "Please, Baba, please?"

"You'll slow us down!" Gege protests. "Besides, you don't even know how to ride."

"Come with us, Baba! Please!" I plead. "Let's all go. Will you take us in your carriage?"

As Baba hesitates, we hear a cough and the unctuous voice of old Ah Wang. "Good morning, Old Master, Young Master and Little Miss," he says, ignoring Ah Zhao as if he doesn't exist. "Teacher Lai has arrived, but Young Master and Little Miss have not had their breakfast yet."

"I'm not hungry," Gege says.

"Nor am I. We don't want any breakfast," I add.

"Tell Teacher Lai to go home," Gege announces airily. "Baba's boss, Commissioner Ye, has ordered us to go shopping today. He's giving Confucius and Mencius a holiday. Instead, Baba's taking everyone to the market in his carriage!"

Baba is obviously in a good mood, because he laughs and waves Ah Wang away.

10

Visit to the Capital

Instead of sitting with Baba and me inside the carriage, Gege insists on joining Ah Zhao and our coachman Little Chen (Xiao Chen 小 陳) on the driver's bench. Baba and I sit side by side in the vehicle. I'm really excited to be going to the city because I'm seldom allowed out of the house. My last outing was three years ago when my grandmother Lao Lao, Niang's mother, died and we buried her in the cemetery.

Although our house is only three *li* 里 (about one mile) from the city gate, the countryside around us is dewy and tranquil. The air smells fresh, trees are turning green and flower buds dot the fields with splashes of color.

As our horses trot past the farms, I see peasants bent over their crops, and men and boys plowing their fields with the help of water buffaloes. On the narrow pathway, our carriage competes for space with goatherds, cow hands and pig farmers shepherding their animals to market. Little Chen wends his way skillfully along the muddy country lane, which soon broadens into a wider road. We pass many small, modest homes as well as a few mansions, similar to ours, before joining the main city highway. The traffic gets heavier as we roll along and we overtake many pedestrians, some carrying heavy loads balanced on shoulder-poles. Farther on, we drive past a train of camels, ox-drawn carts laden with goods, donkeys with animal carcasses or sacks of grain slung across their backs, wheelbarrows, porters staggering under heavy loads, as well as rich men in palanquins and sedan chairs, borne by bearers. Young men on horseback gallop past at high speeds. All of us are headed in the same direction. There's very little traffic going the opposite way.

As we approach the city, the noise around us increases. We hear our coachman's yells intermingled with the sound of horses' hooves, the singsong calls of street vendors and the jingling bells of ox-drawn carts. Our carriage rolls along, weaving deftly between buildings, carts, animals, pedestrians and open stalls. The narrow streets are lined with pottery kilns, artists' studios, iron foundries, shoe-repair stalls and all manner of workshops. I see numerous stands piled high with wine jars, sacks of grain and fresh vegetables.

"Where are we, Baba?"

"We're at the open market, just outside the city proper. Ah Zhao used to work at a store close by the Nine Dragons' Teahouse, next to the river. They serve the best noodles in

Bian Liang, and I happen to have a daughter who loves noodles. . . ."

"Oh, Baba!" I cry. "Are you taking me to a teahouse? I've never set foot in one before."

"Why not? Don't tell your *niang*, that's all. You're still young enough to go to a teahouse with your *baba*. Once a girl gets married, her husband will never allow her to go to such places."

"Married! Who's getting married?"

"You will, one day not too far away!" Baba says, smiling. "Your *niang* has been talking to many matchmakers lately."

Suddenly things start to make sense. This is why Niang has been more interested in the way I look, and this is why she wants me to behave differently. She can see a way of getting rid of me for good.

"But I don't *want* to get married, Baba," I protest. "I'm happy the way I am. Besides, I'm only thirteen years old."

"Come, now— you don't want everyone to accuse your *niang* of neglecting her duty to her daughter, do you? It will lower everyone's respect for her. She needs to arrange a proper marriage for you, and these matters can take time."

My heart sinks, but the idea of marriage seems so ridiculous that it's not difficult to forget all about it. Especially when our carriage turns a corner and we see the Bian River make its dramatic appearance with *Hong Qiao* 虹橋 (the Rainbow Bridge) only a few hundred feet away. The water is thronged with flat-bottomed barges laden with wood, salt, bricks, tiles, coal and sacks of rice. Little Chen brings our vehicle to a halt. He hands the reins to Ah Zhao, hops to the ground and places a footstool for Baba and me to alight.

"You go and get the gourds, Ah Zhao," Baba says. "The three of us are going to the Nine Dragons' Teahouse for lunch."

I can't help feeling sad that Ah Zhao won't be eating with us. Although he's so much more intelligent than Gege and me, he can never be part of our world. No matter how hard he works or how beautifully he carves, he will always be a servant. Why? Because he can't read or write and will never be able to pass the Imperial Examination. How unfair life is! But I know that Baba will not be happy if I say this aloud. So I swallow my words.

The teahouse is situated at a busy crossroads. Baba guides Gege and me around a few donkey carts, porters, sedan chairs and strolling pedestrians. A professional story-teller is entertaining passersby at one corner of the inter-section.

The proprietor himself comes out from the main entrance to greet us and leads us to the second floor. He seats Baba, Gege and me at a square wooden table next to the balcony.

"Window seat for the young lady!" he exclaims.

Through the open window next to me, I have a perfect view of the river. A most delicious aroma of sizzling hot oil and burnt sugar makes our mouths water and our empty stomachs growl.

"*Ma Lao Ban* 馬老板 (Proprietor Ma), I see you are prospering!" Baba says.

"*Zhang Da Ren* 張大人 (Magistrate Zhang)! Thank you

for giving me face by coming to my humble establishment so often. I am greatly honored."

"What are you cooking that smells so good?"

"That's candied fruit, caramelized in hot oil and sautéed with fresh shrimp; a specialty of our establishment."

"Full house again, even though it's so early in the morning. Congratulations! Why work so hard? Stay home and count your money!"

"Your Honor has no idea how difficult life is for me. The people of Bian Liang are impossible to please. Just before you came in, a customer actually scolded me for serving hot dishes today. 'Don't you know it's *Han Shi Jie* 寒食節 (Cold Food Festival) today?' he asked me."

"What's the Cold Food Festival?" Gege asks.

"It's the day before the *Qing Ming Jie* 清明節 (Clear and Bright or Tomb Sweeping Festival)," Baba says. "Tomorrow is Qing Ming."

"Why is it called the Cold Food Festival?"

"Like many of our other festivals, it comes from our history."

"How long ago, Baba? Please tell us," I beg.

"Fifteen hundred years ago, it was the Warring States period and a Duke was fleeing for his life. He ran out of food and was dying of starvation. One of his followers, named Jie, cut off a slice of muscle from his own leg and served it to his master. Eventually, the Duke recovered his health and his throne.

"The Duke decided to appoint Jie to an important post in his cabinet. However, Jie wanted no part of the politics at court. He refused and hid in the mountains instead. The Duke set fire to the region to force him out.

63

"After three days of raging flames, they found Jie's body leaning against a tree, with the corpse of his old mother on his back.

"The Duke was saddened, because he had not meant this to happen. He ordered that from then on, no fires were to be lit for cooking on the anniversary of Jie's death. This is the origin of Cold Food Festival."

"Magistrate Zhang," Proprietor Ma interrupts. "What can we prepare for you today?"

"It's my daughter's first visit to a teahouse. I've told her about your noodles. Let's have an assortment of dishes and some noodles for her. I'll leave the selection to you."

"Right away, Your Honor!"

A waiter brings a pot of hot tea and sets each place at the table with a pair of chopsticks, a porcelain teacup, a plate, a bowl and a spoon. He brings the cold dishes first: sliced ham, tea eggs, preserved tofu and snails with garlic.

After a while, Proprietor Ma himself brings up the hot dishes. "First we have steamed pork ribs flavored with bamboo shoots; next a dish of dumplings filled with minced pork and mushrooms; then stewed duck and cabbage. Finally, another specialty of the house: a big plate of fresh carp from the Bian River, with noodles. Enjoy!"

As we eat, I look out of the window at the river. The Rainbow Bridge is packed with people staring and pointing in one direction over the railing. The bridge is so close I can hear them shouting and see them gesturing in their excitement.

I put my chopsticks down and lean out of the window. A large, flat-bottomed barge is approaching rapidly at an awkward angle. A gust of wind suddenly blows the boat off course, turning it so it's lying almost parallel to the bridge. The crew on board is straining desperately to lower the mast and right the boat against the river's swirling current. The top of the mast looks almost certain to hit the underside of the bridge and cause the boat to capsize. It's very close. The captain yells at his men to row harder. I hold my breath for fear of imminent disaster.

Everyone in the teahouse has stopped eating. The diners converge on my window, pushing and shoving, leaning on me to get a better view. Gege tells them to go away, but they pay no attention. Meanwhile, a huge crowd has gathered along the riverbank to watch the drama. They scream at the captain and shout instructions to the bargemen.

At the last moment, a spectator standing at the apex of the bridge suddenly throws a long coil of rope down to the barge. The sailors reach up with outstretched arms, grab the flying rope and hurriedly tie it to the stern of their ship. Meanwhile, the rest of the crew paddles furiously to turn the craft forward. I hold my breath as the barge lurches precariously, swinging violently from side to side until it finally rights itself. The mast is lowered—just in time—as the vessel slides safely under the bridge to the other side.

Everyone in the teahouse gives a sigh of relief and returns to their seats. Proprietor Ma looks at the food on our table and tells us that it has turned cold. He insists on taking the four hot dishes down to be reheated in the kitchen. While we wait, we see Ah Zhao bounding up the stairs with a big smile on his face.

"Did you see that barge, Old Master? It almost capsized!"

"Were you hoping that it would, you rascal? What are you carrying?" Baba says, smiling.

"Look what I've found!" He pushes our dishes to one side and places a bundle at the center of our table. He unfolds the square piece of cloth and lays out a dazzling assortment of curious objects: several molded-gourd cricket containers, each with a differently carved latticed top made of tortoiseshell, bamboo, horn or wood; a porcelain feeding tray; clay pots and fighting arenas; tweezers for grooming; a double bamboo cage, made for two crickets, with a single handle and a sliding divider in the middle; a dome-shaped, pocket-sized brass carrier covered by wire mesh; a sandalwood tube with a breathing cover and feeder at the bottom; and a tickler with fine hairs sprouting from a bamboo handle.

"What sort of hair do they use to make these cricket ticklers? They're so fine! Almost invisible." Gege tilts his head back and inserts the tickler into his right nostril. He twirls the handle, screws up his face and gives a violent sneeze.

"*Ah-cheoow!*" Gege exclaims. "Ready for a song or a fight, anyone? No? How about a little tickle up the nose and a good sneeze instead? By the way, you never answered me. What sort of hair is this?"

"If you really want to know, these fine hairs are rats' whiskers!"

"Rats' whiskers! *Ah yah!* Why didn't you tell me before? How do I rinse out my nostril?"

"Did you buy all this cricket paraphernalia, Ah Zhao?" Baba asks.

"Of course not, Old Master! I thought you might like to

see everything, that's all. Aren't they interesting? Whatever you don't want, I'll return."

"These gourds are beautiful," Baba says, picking one up. "Especially this one. They're all different, aren't they?"

"You can say *that* again. Some gourds have smaller turns, while others have larger turns than their bellies. The ones with long, slender necks are called goose-necks. The fat, round, shiny ones are called monk-heads. The one you have in your hand has a pointed bottom. It's called a spider-bellied gourd."

"I really like this one," Baba says, taking off the gourd's latticed tortoiseshell top and peering into its interior. "It's beautifully proportioned. Inside, it has a thick rind, which will maintain an even temperature for our cricket lodger."

"Old Master! You have excellent taste. That one's my favorite too. Look at the glossy patina on its surface! According to the dealer, the patina is from years of being caressed by numerous previous owners. He says this gourd is an antique from the Tang Dynasty. It's at least three hundred years old."

At that moment, Proprietor Ma appears with a tray of steaming dishes, and the delicious aroma of fresh carp, pork ribs and bamboo shoots fills the air. Ah Zhao hurriedly repacks his assortment of cricket-ware and prepares to leave.

"Buy the antique gourd and that fat, round, shiny one you call monk-head. Bargain for a good price," Baba says.

"Tell them to throw in the tickler!" Gege adds.

"Do you need some more money?" Baba asks.

"The string of cash you gave me earlier is more than enough."

67

Baba reaches into the voluminous sleeve of his robe and takes out a few more coins. "Here, this is lunch money for you and Little Chen."

"Thank you, Old Master." Ah Zhao bows. "We're going to watch the preparations for the Qing Ming Festival, but we won't be far away."

"What's the Qing Ming Festival, Baba?" I ask.

"That's a day for us to remember our ancestors. About four hundred years ago, one of the Tang Emperors declared that the day following the Cold Food Festival should be named Qing Ming Jie (Clear and Bright Festival). Nowadays we combine the two holidays together into a joined Qing Ming Festival for sweeping our ancestors' tombs."

"And also for playing games," Gege adds. "I remember one Qing Ming Festival when you took me to Ye Ye's 爺爺 (Grandfather's) tomb and we had a picnic. Afterward we played tug-of-war and *cu ju* 蹴鞠 (football) and flew kites. It was such a fun day."

"How come *I* didn't get to go there for Qing Ming, Baba?" I ask.

"That was the year I took your brother to see my old house in Shandong Province, where your *ye ye* is buried," Baba says. "It's too far for you to travel. Girls shouldn't get out of the house too often. . . . Besides, your *niang* doesn't like to leave her room. We haven't celebrated Qing Ming for many years now."

Along the River
at Qing Ming

Proprietor Ma comes up to Baba toward the end of lunch and asks to speak to him privately.

"How long will it take?"

"It's about your investment in my humble establishment. I need to show you the books. It might take a while. Do you have time?"

"I have time, but what about my children?"

"Today's the beginning of Qing Ming. Have you not seen the crowds? So many things to do and see. They can walk around the marketplace, fly kites, go on a boat ride, even enter the city to watch the jugglers, or have their fortunes told."

"Oh, Baba," I cry. "Please let Gege show me everything!"

Baba smiles indulgently and reaches into his sleeve. "Here are some coins. Tell Ah Zhao to accompany you. He knows the city well."

"What if you're finished before us?" I ask.

"That's a good point ... hmm ..." Baba strokes his beard and looks at our excited faces. "Tell you what: since this is Little Sister's first visit to the city, why don't you tell Little Chen to wait for you and drive you home? When I'm done, I'll just hire a sedan chair and go home on my own."

Gege runs downstairs in high spirits, taking the steps two at a time, as usual. I follow more slowly, as stairs are always tricky for my toes, some of which do not bend. He turns around impatiently and tells me to hurry.

Outside, the sun is blazing and the weather is turning warm. In front of us is the dazzling river. As far as I can see, its entire length is dotted with boats of all varieties, sizes and colors. There are flat-bottomed transport barges laden with sacks of grain, ferries packed with passengers, tiny rowing boats close to shore, river rafts, giant merchant ships and small sampans flying past at high speed. Everyone is going to or arriving from somewhere else. I suddenly realize how narrow my world is.

We find Little Chen fast asleep by the side of the carriage. Ah Zhao is a little distance away, talking animatedly to a stallkeeper. A blue flag with the single word *niao* 鳥 (bird) written in red is flying in the breeze. As we approach, I see a small crowd of people gathered round the stallkeeper. He's standing in front of a number of bamboo cages, each containing a single bird.

"I've never heard of such a thing," the bird-seller is saying. "The price of one of these sparrow hawks alone is twenty *tong bi* 銅幣 (copper coins). How can I sell you this stack of three birds for ten coppers?"

"I'm not particular about what kind of bird it is," Ah Zhao replies. "Just let me have any three birds for ten coppers. In fact, you can even keep your cages if—"

"What about getting the sparrow hawk? This one is trained to hunt."

The merchant takes the black-and-white bird out of its cage and places it on his left forearm. He points to a sparrow hopping around from stall to stall, then coaxes the hawk into a lying-down position on his right palm. Immediately, the hawk's eyes rivet on the sparrow.

"Give me fifteen copper coins and I'll show you how to throw my hawk at that sparrow like a dart. If it doesn't kill its quarry with one try, you can have your money back and take any one of my birds home for free. If it succeeds, I keep the money and this sparrow hawk is yours. How about it?"

"No! I loathe birds that hunt!" Ah Zhao says. "Give me three birds for ten coppers and keep your cages."

"I never heard of such a thing! How're you going to take the birds home without their cages?"

"That's my problem. Not yours."

"I'll go bankrupt if I sell you three birds for ten coppers."

"All right! How about two birds for ten coppers?"

"Who keeps the cages?"

"You do."

"Any type of birds?"

"Yes."

"How about these two pigeons for ten coppers?"

"Fine!"

"So, these two pigeons are yours for ten coppers. Now, I'd like to see what you're going to do with them without a cage."

He hands over the two caged birds to Ah Zhao, who pays him. Ah Zhao calmly opens the doors of the cages and releases the pigeons, one after the other, into the sky. A murmur of astonishment goes through the crowd of onlookers. I can tell by the way they shake their heads that they can hardly believe what they are seeing.

The bird-seller is outraged. "What did you do *that* for?"

"If you were a bird imprisoned in a cage, what's the one thing you would yearn for?"

"I have no idea. What is it?"

"Freedom! Lack of freedom is a fate worse than death!"

"You're mad! But why should I care? Just give me back my cages, as agreed, and we'll go our separate ways."

I watch as the two pigeons flap their wings and soar away joyously toward the horizon. Happy birds, I think to myself. I wish I had eyes buried in their feathers so I could follow their flight across the wide blue yonder and go wherever they roam. I can see from Ah Zhao's body language that he's happy to have set the birds free. It occurs to me that, as a servant, he must feel like a caged bird himself. Just like me.

At that moment, Gege creeps up stealthily behind Ah Zhao, tackles him from behind, covers his eyes and shouts, "Guess who I am, Big Nose!"

"Can it possibly be the handsome and talented Zhang Ze Duan, famous court-painter-to-be?" The two boys laugh and shadowbox and chase one another along the grassy shore.

"Tell me about the boats, Ah Zhao," I say.

"Amazing variety, aren't they?" He brushes grass off his black, hemp cloth trousers as I join them. "See the cluster of boats on the other side of the teahouse? Most of those belong to fishermen. Families of four or six people sleep, eat and work in them."

"I see some fishermen even keep birds as pets."

"Those are special birds called cormorants. The fisherman places a metal ring round their neck so they can't swallow big fish. He lowers them into the water to catch fish, then takes the ones they can't swallow from their mouths."

"What about that cargo boat laden with boxes? What's making it move up the river?" Gege points to two vessels close together, one behind the other. "I don't see any sails or oars, let alone anyone rowing."

"That's because the smaller boat in front is a paddle-wheeled tugboat. Instead of sails or oars, these wooden paddle wheels are moving the two boats forward."

"How about those two big boats docked along the banks to our right? Are the workers loading or unloading?"

"Who knows? The one with multiple decks that looks like a big house may be a merchant ship. Both of them are big enough to sail to the ocean or to other countries. See those gigantic masts? When all the sails are pulled up they look like great clouds in the sky."

"What are the sails made of?"

"Bamboo matting. The sailors probably took some of them down for cleaning and repairs. The direction of those sails can be changed from moment to moment to catch the wind. That way, the sailors can go wherever they wish."

"How glorious! To go wherever one wishes!" Gege says longingly.

"Wouldn't it be wonderful if the three of us could board one of those boats and sail somewhere far, far away?" I say, mesmerized by the panoramic view and the possibility of travel.

"How I long to be a sailor!" Gege exclaims. "I simply hate my lessons! As for those ancient books I have to learn by heart, I don't know anyone who speaks like that. Why should I waste my time? Let's run away instead!"

"How will we support ourselves?" Ah Zhao says.

"You can teach us how to paint, and we'll sell our paintings. Or else we can stage cricket fights and make bets!"

"What sort of life is that? You two have no idea what it's like out there."

"Show us!" I cry. "I want to see everything, today!"

"See everything in one afternoon? How much time do you have? Where's your *baba*?"

"Baba says he'll go home by himself," Gege says. "We need to wake up Little Chen and tell him to wait here and take us home later. We have the whole day ahead of us."

"Let's get started!" I shout, giddy with excitement. "This is the first time I've been out of the house without my parents. I want to see everything!"

"Follow me!" Ah Zhao says. "With so much free time, *you he bu ke* 有何不可 (is anything impossible)?"

Two queues stretch in front of the gate: a long line to the right for carriages and carts, and a much shorter line to the left for pedestrians, peddlers and riders. As we approach, the imposing city gate appears to grow taller and taller, looming up to a height of at least thirty men (approximately fifteen *zhang* 丈). The name of our capital city, Bian Liang 汴梁, is written in beautiful, giant calligraphy and prominently displayed on a gold placard hanging from the roof of the building above the gate.

Facing us are two sets of rectangular doors, one behind the other, each two *zhang* high. The outer door is made of a single thick sheet of iron. It's controlled by heavy chains that hoist the door up or down; the inner double door is made of carved wood and opens inward. Above the doors is a traditional administration building, with flying eaves and upturned corners, enclosed by a balcony. Steep stone steps lead from the top of the wall to the building's entrance. Parapets along the top of the wall act as lookout towers during times of trouble and provide shelter for archers to shoot arrows.

A black-robed ticket official sits at a table inside the gate, counting coins with the help of a *suan pan* 算盤 (abacus) and logging the sum into a ledger with brush and ink. He stamps a sheet of paper firmly with his *tu zhang* 圖章 (chop or seal), gives it to the driver standing at his desk and waves him on before beckoning to the next driver to come forward.

We queue behind a troupe of musicians dressed in black costumes with red sashes round their waists. They are carrying their musical instruments: bamboo flutes, reed pipes, drums, *erhu* 二胡 (two-stringed fiddle), *qin* 琴 (zither), lute, cymbals and bells.

"Carriages and carts have to pay tolls to go through the

gate," says one musician to another, "but pedestrians get in for free during the Qing Ming Festival."

Gege taps the musician on his arm to get his attention. "Where will you be performing?"

"At the Longevity Gardens. There's going to be a kite-flying competition this afternoon. You three should come and join the fun. It's only half a *li* upriver to your left. We're going to have a hot and noisy party."

"When do the city gates close?" I ask.

"At sundown."

"Don't worry about that," Ah Zhao interrupts. "You'll hear the drums."

"Drums?" I ask. "What drums?"

"See the ornate guardhouse standing atop the city gates?" the musician says. "There's a bell as well as a drum in that guardhouse. The bell is rung at sunrise every morning, when the city gates open, and the drum is beaten at sundown every evening, to warn you the gates are about to close."

"How many bells and drums are there altogether?"

"The city wall has twelve separate gates," Ah Zhao says, "but I'm not sure whether each gate has a bell and drum in its guardhouse."

"Don't worry," the musician says. "Unless you're deaf, you're bound to hear the drums at sundown. You'll know when to get out."

Inside the walled city there are even more people milling about: tightrope-walkers, pole acts, jugglers, clowns, fortune-tellers, actors and professional storytellers are all surrounded by dense crowds. We walk past a barbershop and see a bearded man being shaved with a sharp, curved knife. Down the street a well-muscled army officer is testing the suppleness of a crossbow at an archery stall. Next to him, illiterate farmers wait patiently for a public scribe to write their letters for a fee.

We mingle with shoppers, beggars, monks asking for alms, and families out on holiday. I can't help laughing at a bare-bottomed little boy who's trying to climb into a peddler's basket. A sign on the basket proclaims that the peddler can cure diseases of cows and horses, as well as children! Many people are dressed in their best holiday clothes, with elaborate headgear. It's so noisy we can hardly hear one another speak. Suddenly a loud bang startles me, but Ah Zhao says it's just a firecracker. I'm fascinated by all the different shops and restaurants, hotels, temples, official buildings and private residences, ranging from modest dwellings to grand mansions with meticulously maintained yards.

Gege and Ah Zhao walk on either side of me to make sure that I don't get lost in the crowd. As we stroll along the riverbank, toward the Longevity Gardens, the crowds thin out a little and I see hundreds of paper kites, shaped like birds and butterflies, flying in the wind. Some are tied to long poles wrapped in colorful silk banners, all bearing the characters 清明風箏節 *Qing Ming Feng Zheng Jie* (Qing Ming Kite Festival).

The Longevity Gardens turn out to be a large, empty field on a raised plateau overlooking the river on one side, and plots of vegetables and wheat on the other. The best thing about the grounds is the panoramic view of the city of Bian Liang. The three of us stand at the edge of the plateau, with Gege in the middle. He drapes his arms affectionately around our shoulders.

"When we get home," Gege says, "I'm going to paint a picture of this great scene, exactly as it is at this moment. I'll remember how it looks right now and never let go of the image. Will you help me do this, Big Nose?"

"Of course—we'll do it together! We need to make the river the centerpiece of your painting. Be sure to remember the direction of the sun; we'll put in sunshine and shadows where we see them now."

"How do you draw sunshine?"

"When you draw dark shadows, the spaces you leave blank will be sunshine."

"Brilliant! We'll name the painting *Along the River at Qing Ming*. It will preserve a slice of Bian Liang city life, during Emperor Huizong's reign, for our grandchildren and our great-great-grandchildren."

"There's something mysterious about this river, isn't there?" I muse.

"I know," Ah Zhao agrees. "Where does it begin and where does it end? I want to follow it to its source and find out."

"And I want something to eat," Gege says, bringing us back to earth.

At the edge of the field are stands selling hot and cold drinks, noodles, dumplings and steamed buns. Gege buys us each a bun. I bite into the fluffy, light exterior, waiting for the meat and the hot, savory juices to run over my tongue. It tastes so good that I ask for another, but I can't finish it, so the boys share it.

We pass a large stall piled high with kites of different shapes and sizes, each more colorful than the last. Some are tied to poles so that they billow in the wind. Most are made of paper, but a few are silk. I can't resist touching one shaped like a bird with orange-and-yellow wings, green tail and blue body.

"This kite is yours for only eight coppers," the toothless old kite merchant says to me. "Today is a perfect day for kite-flying. Neither too hot nor too cold. Nice breeze blowing, but not too strong. See the leaves rustling in the treetops, and the flags flying on that big boat over there? All indicators of good kite-flying weather. On top of that, not a hint of rain, so you won't be troubled by lightning."

"What's this kite made of?"

"Bamboo frame, paper sail and silk flying line. Silk kites are much more expensive. We carry both kinds. Our special kites look like insects, butterflies, dragons, fish and other animals. Our musical kites have flutes, gourds or bows attached to them, so the wind 'plays' musical tunes as the kites fly."

"What about this one?" Gege asks, pointing to a small diamond-shaped kite attached to a line coated with shards of metal.

"That's a fighter kite, made for boys. Buy two of them. Then you and your friend can have a friendly contest trying to cut one another's lines. But be careful that you don't injure your hands while handling the lines."

* * *

A dizzying variety of competitions are being held at different areas of the field. There's a group of small children tripping along, trailing small paper kites. Someone in the distance is counting out numbers in clear, measured tones: ". . . forty-two, forty-three, forty-four . . ." The majority of the kites flutter and crash before the announcer reaches one hundred. One little girl with two pigtails pointing upward bursts into tears as her kite blows away in the wind.

Farther along is a group of teenagers about our age. One of them has managed to raise his kite to a height over five hundred *zhang*.

I see an elderly man handling a butterfly kite so skillfully that it looks alive. He steers it with two lines of equal length strapped to his wrists. His kite can dance, fly loop-the-loop, turn somersaults in the air, or dive down before swooping back gracefully towards the sky.

Next to him is a team of eight men assembling a giant red-and-brown dragon-shaped kite with a long tail. It's an elaborate affair with many bamboo hinges and numerous strings joined together into a single line attached to a handle and wheel. The team leader studies the wind direction and tells his men where to stand. At just the right moment, he barks out an order. Everyone dashes forward with the kite raised above their heads. As the dragon inflates with wind, the leader signals its release. The kite rises with grace, floating majestically into the sky, while the leader hastily pays out extra lengths of string from his wheel. It doesn't take long for the dragon to rise to a great height, swaying and swerving as if it's alive.

To our left, men and boys are shouting, cheering and chasing one another in an area away from the kite-flyers.

It's a large, flat, rectangular field marked off with a red rope.

"*Cu ju* (football)!" Gege exclaims, in great excitement, and races ahead. When Ah Zhao and I finally catch up, he's already among the players, chasing after a large brown leather ball.

Two young men approach us with friendly smiles as we watch the ball being kicked from player to player.

"Ever played *cu ju* before?"

"No," Ah Zhao says. "How do you play?"

"Easy. You can touch the ball with any part of your body except your hands. See those two posts in the middle of the field with netting between them? That's the goal. We divide the players into two teams by giving you red or black head-bands with numbers on them. Red team scores one point if a Red player kicks the ball into the goal facing the Red side of the field. Same goes for Black. Everyone aims to score as many points as possible while preventing the other side from scoring."

"How much does it cost to play?"

"We charge a small fee. But why don't you start playing first, so we can observe you? If you're talented, we might even ask you to join our organization and pay you for play-ing!"

"That will be the day!" Ah Zhao says, laughing and turning to me. "Feel like trying?"

I'm sorely tempted, but I can't run fast, so I shake my head.

"Are girls allowed to play?" Ah Zhao asks.

"Of course they are! During the Tang Dynasty, there was a seventeen-year-old girl who was so talented she beat a team made up of army soldiers. If you feel like playing, just signal us."

Meanwhile, Gege is darting about wearing a Red head-band with the number *shi er* 十二 (twelve) on his forehead. A scoreboard on top of the goalposts shows the score tied at one all. A tall and lanky lad wearing Black number *ba* 八 (eight) takes the ball near midfield and fires from long range. The stocky goalkeeper, Red number *wu* 五 (five), blocks the shot and kicks it out to Red number twelve (Gege!), who chases it down and passes it to Red number *san* 三 (three). Number three handles the ball nimbly backward and forward between his feet, gets behind the Black defense and fires a shot that rebounds off the Black team's goalpost. The entire Red team groans with disappointment.

"From the way he kicks the ball, I think your brother must have played *cu ju* before," Ah Zhao says.

"But where?"

"There are many *cu ju* fields like this throughout Bian Liang. I even saw one in the backyard at Commissioner Ye's house."

"How long do you think Gege will play?"

"I won't be surprised if he's here until sundown. Let him enjoy himself. I'll tell the organizers that we'll wait for him at the riverbank below."

The weather grows even hotter as we saunter down the plateau toward the river. Snatches of music drift toward us, mingled with shouts and peals of laughter. We meander down a grassy slope and enter a narrow stone passageway flanked by feathery maples, lush flowering shrubs and tow-

82

ering bamboos. Below us, a green meadow stretches all the way to the river. A graveled walkway shaded by graceful willows runs along the riverbank. Nestled within the blue-green haze of leafy willow branches is a little wooden bench flanked by two pear trees ablaze with fragrant yellow flowers.

Ah Zhao leads me to the bench and signals me to sit.

"What about you?" I ask.

"That's not for the likes of me," he says with a hint of darkness. "You're the boss and I'm the slave. Let's remember this at all times."

He picks up a flat stone from the path and throws it toward the water with such force that it skips the surface three times before it sinks. I wonder what has happened to change his mood.

"It's so beautiful and tranquil here. Why isn't anyone around?"

"Maybe they don't know about it."

"How lucky we are!"

"Are we?" he asks moodily, staring into the distance. After a while, he walks toward the water and climbs onto a little barge moored there. Sitting at the edge, he removes his shoes, puts his feet into the cool river and begins to hum a strange tune.

It suddenly strikes me that he's handsome, despite his crooked nose. Starting with his height, his muscled frame, his light skin, his curly black hair, his long-lashed, deep-set eyes and ending with his nose . . . I think of his nickname, Big Nose, and say to myself, "His nose isn't really big. It's tall rather than big."

"Why are you staring at me?"

His question catches me off guard. I lower my eyes, but I know my face must be turning red.

"I'm just thinking that your nose is tall rather than big. Your nickname should be *Gao Bi Zi* 高鼻子 (Tall Nose), not *Da Bi Zi* (Big Nose)."

"Am I really that different from everyone else? Why give me a nickname at all? Don't I eat, drink and breathe just like you? Are we that dissimilar?"

"Of course not! Actually, I was thinking that your face is more interesting than mine. Or Gege's. It's more three-dimensional."

"Interesting!" He spits out the word with loathing. "Interesting indeed. Am I an animal in a zoo? To be gawked at and compared to human beings?"

"Why are you getting angry?"

He looks away, and for a while he says nothing. Then I see tears coursing down his cheeks and I realize he's crying.

Something comes over me. Even though he's tall and strong, at that moment he looks like a little lost boy and I think of him alone in the world with nobody to turn to. Without thinking, I climb onto the barge, sit down next to him, take off my shoes and dangle my bare feet in the river. The cool water feels delicious against my skin as I wriggle my toes. Neither of us says anything for a while. A million thoughts race through my mind.

"Why are the toes on your right foot so crooked?" His question makes me jump. Instinctively, I bend my foot back to hide my ugly toes.

"Did you have an accident?" he persists.

"No, I did not."

"Are your crooked toes the reason why you wouldn't play *cu ju* just now?"

"How did you know?"

"I know, that's all. . . ."

There's a long silence. Then I say, "Can you and I truly be friends?"

"Not if you don't tell me anything about yourself. Besides, are you sure you want to be friends with someone like me? A servant?"

"Yes! You're the smartest person I know."

"Friends don't have secrets from one another."

"I agree . . . but there's a lot I don't know about you."

"That's because there's nothing to tell."

"Oh, sorry—what was that about friends not having secrets . . . ?"

"I'm serious. What is there to tell? I'm an orphan. My father was a barbarian who couldn't read or write. My mother died the same day I was born."

"Where are you from?"

"You mean, where am I *really* from. My father's parents were Jews. My grandfather's name used to be Levy, but he changed it to Li after they moved here. When he was a little boy, my father traveled across the desert with my grandparents, to come to China. He used to tell me about the vastness of the desert . . . the sand dunes stretching on and on as far as the eye could see . . . the searing sun during the day and the black, freezing nights . . . the miraculous sunsets and fantastic sunrises . . . the terrifying forays into the nothingness to search for water . . . the endless silence . . . They came from a foreign country far away to the west, *tian xia zhi bian yuan* 天下之邊緣 (at the edge of civilization). My grandparents disowned my father after he married my Chinese mother. Throughout his life, my father felt that he didn't belong here . . . or anywhere. Sometimes I feel that I need to search for the places where my father lived before he came to China. I have this strong desire to travel, to retrieve my lost heritage."

"What did your *baba* do?"

"He was a laborer . . . a carpenter and stonecutter. After my mama died, my *baba* was alone in a strange land. He found it difficult to get work, and over the years he got depressed and angry. He used to gamble what money he had. Just before he died, he placed huge bets on a cricket he believed in. At first it won, but eventually it lost. Baba accused his opponent of cheating. They fought and my *baba* was stabbed to death."

I try to imagine what it would be like to have no parents, but I can't. I feel a deep sadness for Ah Zhao as I realize how alone he is.

"Why have you never told me all this before?"

"You've never asked. To you, and the rest of your family, I'm not even a regular person, let alone a friend. I'm merely the barbarian hedge-clipper and tree-trimmer. I am, and will always be, a *wai ren* 外人 (outsider)."

"That's not true! You and I have become friends, and now you won't be alone anymore."

"All right, friend! It's your turn now to share. Tell me how your toes got broken."

I close my eyes and fight the feeling of nausea that always comes when I think about that day.

"My *niang* . . . my *niang* . . ."

Tears come to my eyes, and I look down and try to control myself.

Ah Zhao leans over and looks into my face. "I'm sorry—I didn't want to upset you. Don't tell me any more if you'd rather not."

After a while, the sickness goes and I find that I do want to talk about that terrible day, long ago. I take a deep breath and begin.

12

Mei Lan's Confession

"Since I was a toddler, and for as long as I can remember," I tell Ah Zhao, "I'd heard Niang speaking to Baba about choosing an auspicious day to bind my feet. She spoke of my foot-binding as a momentous and special occasion; a sort of combined feast day/name day/celebration holiday when I would shed the cocoon of my infancy and turn into Mei Lan (Beautiful Orchid). I would become as lovely as my *niang*.

"She told Baba and me that all her wealthy friends were binding their daughters' feet, and that only poor peasant girls ended up with big, ugly, natural feet these days. My bound feet would announce to the world that I have a wealthy father and far-sighted mother. Matchmakers would be clamoring to represent me.

"I had no idea what foot-binding involved, but I couldn't wait to be as beautiful as Niang!

"In those days I thought she loved me.

"In the autumn of the Year of the Ox (1097), when I was six years old, an important monk came from the Buddhist Temple to our house in a palanquin carried by four young apprentices. All five men had shaven heads and were dressed in coarse brown robes. Baba welcomed the chief monk into our parlour while the others waited outside.

"Niang didn't meet the monk face-to-face, but she was behind the latticed screen that divides the room into two. You know the screen I'm talking about . . . it's still there, and was made in such a way that Baba and the monk could not see her, but Niang was able to see and hear them. As a special favor, Niang said I could stay there with her.

"I peeped eagerly through the holes in the screen, and watched Baba and the monk take their seats, across from one another, on high-backed hardwood chairs covered with red cushions. Between them was a square wooden table with two cups of tea and a large bowl of tangerines. A tiger-skin rug lay under the table.

"I could see steam rising from the hot tea as Baba took the lid off the cup. He raised the teacup with both hands and bowed his head slightly.

"The monk took the lid off his cup and bowed in return, before taking a sip.

"'Everything has its time and place,' the monk said, 'including the auspicious date of your daughter's foot-binding. During the past month, we have spent a lot of time figuring out her *Ba Zi* 八字 (Eight Characters).'

89

" 'For the sake of my wife, who is behind the screen, will you explain the concept of Eight Characters?'

"The monk smiled.

" 'What is the most important thing that determines a person's life?' he asked.

" 'Tell me!'

" 'It's luck. You are who you are today because of your luck. And I am who I am because of my luck. By combining your daughter's Eight Characters with my astrological knowledge of *feng shui* 風水 (fortune), I'll be able to find on my abacus the most auspicious day for her foot-binding.'

"My heart quickened. They were finally talking about my foot-binding!

" 'What *is* Eight Characters?' I whispered to Niang.

"She placed her finger against her lips to silence me and mouthed the word, 'Listen.'

" 'Is the concept of Eight Characters the same as the Four Pillars of Life?' Baba was asking.

" 'They are one and the same. The Four Pillars of your daughter's life consist of the year, month, day and time of her birth. Each Pillar consists of two words. Four times two equals eight. Hence the term Four Pillars is also known as Eight Words or Eight Characters.'

" 'So the year, month, day and time of a person's birth determine his fate!' Baba mused. 'But thousands of babies are born on the same day at the same hour. Do they end up with the same fate?'

" 'Of course not! That's where my knowledge of Chinese astrology and *feng shui* comes in. Other factors must be taken into account, such as place of birth, family background, education and behaviour. My calculations are based on ancient wisdom handed down to me by my teachers, who learnt it from their teachers, and so on over many, many generations.'

" 'What do you use your abacus for?'

" '*Feng shui* depends on precise mathematical calculations. It's not a guessing game. To find the right day for your daughter's foot-binding, I need to plug in *Yin* 陰 and *Yang* 陽, the *Wu Xing* 五行 (Five Elements) and the *Shi Er Sheng Xiao* 十二生肖 (Twelve Animals of the Zodiac: rat, ox, tiger, rabbit, dragon, snake, horse, goat, monkey, rooster, dog and pig). In addition, her fate is also determined by the position of the sun, moon, planets and comets at the exact time and place of her birth.'

"At this moment, Niang signaled that we should leave, but later that day, Baba came to my room and handed me a large red envelope with my name, Zhang Mei Lan 張美蘭, written in beautiful calligraphy. In it were two sheets of red paper. The first was a chart divided into four columns. Each column was filled with difficult words that I didn't recognize. The second sheet had only six characters: 十月八日, 牛年.

" 'What do these characters on the first page say, Baba?'

" 'That's your *feng shui* according to your Eight Characters. Can you read the words on the second page?'

" 'Yes, Baba! It says Eighth Day of the Tenth Moon, Year of the Ox.'

" 'That is the auspicious day of your foot-binding. Eighth Day of the Tenth Moon, Year of the Ox.'

"I couldn't wait, but finally the day arrived. Niang got up

early and woke Nai Ma and me. This was highly unusual because normally she slept until lunchtime. Niang seemed happy and excited as she ordered Nai Ma to bring jugs of hot water. In her hands she held a basin in which were two rolls of bandages, a large towel, a pair of scissors, some needles and thread. She and Nai Ma bathed me and cut my toenails. Then they soaked my feet in the basin of water before massaging them.

"I could see that Nai Ma wasn't sure what to do next without instructions from Niang. I couldn't understand why she looked so nervous. Her hands were trembling and she avoided my eyes.

"I wanted to reassure Nai Ma that I was feeling marvellous. It was truly relaxing to have my toes rubbed and my feet massaged, especially by my Niang. The two of them went on for so long that I almost fell asleep.

"Then Niang pulled out a long, narrow bandage. She ordered Nai Ma to hold on to my right foot and not let go even if I should try to free myself.

"This made me laugh. I wanted to reassure them. 'Don't worry!' I said. 'I promise I won't move. Why should I free myself? I *want* to have my feet bound. I want small, beautiful feet just like yours, Niang.'

"Neither of them said anything, but Nai Ma was now looking at me with an expression I've never seen before.

"Slowly and carefully, Niang wound the narrow piece of cloth round my four smaller toes, leaving my big toe bare. Next, she pulled the bandage tightly around my instep, heel and ankle. Then she looped the cloth back over my toes, wrapping it around my foot and ankle five times. My foot felt tight and hot, but it was not unbearable. Niang eyed the bandage in her hand as she paused.

"'Is it all over?' I asked hopefully. 'I *told* you I wouldn't move!'

"Neither of them answered. Nai Ma held my leg more firmly. Niang looked her in the eye.

"'One. Two. Three. Now!' Niang commanded in a firm voice. With both of Niang's hands pushing my four smaller toes down towards the sole of my foot, Nai Ma began pulling the bandage as tightly as possible. The worst pain I had ever experienced shot from my toes throughout my entire body. I realized with sudden shock that Niang was trying to bend my toes under my sole, no matter what. Even if it meant breaking my bones.

"Despite my promise to be good, I screamed. Niang went on pushing. I felt a jolt of excruciating agony as my toes fractured under their combined assault. I heard them snap and I could not believe that anyone could do this. I kicked and struggled, but they went on relentlessly pulling the bandages tighter and tighter. It hurt so much that I wet myself and vomited. I simply couldn't help myself. Darts of pain shot up my leg into my chest. Surely death could not be worse than this.

"At that moment I saw with absolute clarity that the cause of Niang's long-standing illness was connected somehow to her small, bound feet. She must have gone through the same torture she was inflicting on me at this moment. She knew what it was like, and she didn't protect me. If the result of enduring all this was to lie in bed like her for the rest of my life, I wanted no part of it. No matter how beautiful it made me!

"I bit my lower lip until it bled and made up my mind to fight. I punched and scratched and kicked at Niang with my left foot as hard as I could. I pulled Nai Ma's hair as she bent down to speak to me.

"'Stop it!' I screamed. '*I don't want my feet bound!* You're hurting me!'

"'I'm sorry,' Nai Ma said. 'Your Niang is doing this for your future.' As she spoke, she loosened her hold on my leg just for a second and I wriggled free.

"I sprang from the bed, pushed Niang to the floor and scrambled frantically out of my room. I ran, regardless of the pain, with the bandage trailing behind me like a twisting, twirling snake. Down the hall, through the threshold of the main doorway and into the courtyard where there were people . . . lots of people . . . and safety . . . and freedom.

"Baba was standing by his sedan chair, talking to the bearers and Gege about a broken shoulder-pole. On the far side, two gardeners were emptying buckets of water into spraying cans. How could everything be so normal when I was being tortured?

"'Save me! Baba! Save my life! She's trying to kill me!' I hollered at the top of my lungs. Tears streamed down my face as I threw myself into Baba's arms.

"Everyone stopped to stare at me.

"'Who is trying to kill you?' Baba asked

"'Niang!'

"'Don't be ridiculous! She's your mother.'

"'No! She's not my mother. She's my stepmother! Look what she's done!'

"I ripped off my bandage and raised my foot to show

94

him. My foot began to swell before our very eyes. It changed color from white to yellow to red to purple. My toes were hanging at a grotesque angle, all the bones having been cracked and broken. The only toe that appeared normal was my big toe, pointing straight out and reminding me of how my foot used to look a short while ago.

"Baba was horrified! Everyone rushed over to look. A murmur went through the crowd. I heard someone say, 'How could she have run when four of her toes are fractured like this?'

"Gege knelt beside me and took my throbbing foot in his hands. I knew he felt bad for me because I saw tears in his eyes. Gently, he stroked my little toe and tried to straighten it. The pain was so excruciating that I screamed again."

"My relationship with Niang never recovered after this. Nor did the toes in my foot. The fractures healed, but my toes remained crooked, summoning up my ordeal each time I put on my shoes. A few months later, Baba spoke to me vaguely about hiring a professional foot-binder to bind my feet. I told him I would stop eating and drinking if he forced me to submit to this torture again. The whole matter of my foot-binding became a contest of wills between the three of us. Eventually, Baba must have sided with me, because my feet remained unbound. But Niang never forgave me, and from that time on she deliberately made my life as difficult as possible—but only if we were alone. When my father was around, she was as sweet as honey, but the memory of what happened on that 'auspicious' day lingered on between us like a stinky fart.

"I tried to talk to Nai Ma, but she refused to discuss it.

For once, she was unsympathetic and stubborn. Since there was nobody to talk to, I described the incident to myself in my notebook. I felt much better afterwards. From then on, I began writing whenever I had a spare moment.

"So now you know everything. Niang broke my toes, but I got away. That's why I have big, ugly feet," I said defiantly.

"Your feet are not ugly," said Ah Zhao, looking into my eyes. "They're beautiful, just like the rest of you. Is it permissible for a servant to tell his master's daughter that she's beautiful?"

A pang goes through me when I hear him, and I start to tremble. "Don't say such things!"

"You're right! I should not have said that to you . . . but, surely, even a servant has eyes? Seeing is knowledge. What we see remains with us. One day, I'll paint the images I'm carrying in my mind. That way, even though I have no home, I'll create one wherever I go."

I think of our "playroom" and know in my heart that neither Gege nor I could have built it without him. What he says is true. He'll be able to effect his sanctuary wherever he goes; establish an oasis where things come together; install a tranquil retreat at will. But we, the ones left behind, will be lost without him. . . .

At that moment, a curious, pounding noise suddenly starts up as if from nowhere. Muted, rhythmic and insistent, the ominous beat grows louder and louder: Boom, boom, boom, boom, *boom!* Boom, boom, boom, boom, *boom!*

"What's that?" I ask in alarm.

"Remember the Bell and Drum Tower in the guardhouse

above the city gates? They're beating the drums to warn us that the gates are about to close for the evening."

"Sundown already?"

"I'm afraid so. Time to go."

We make our way back to the plateau above the riverbank and gaze at the peaceful city of Bian Liang spread out below. Around the entire length of the shore, as far as the eye can see, mile after mile of cultivated fields, hamlets, orchards, markets, roads, bridges, canals and boats are laid out like toys in a playland, under the setting sun. The expanse of blue river, flowing from west to east, seems almost endless. A line of red stretches like a gentle brushstroke across the darkening sky.

Ah Zhao and I wave to Gege. He leaves his *cu ju* friends and runs toward us, the personification of life and hope. My heart vibrates with the magic of youth and I'm suddenly infused with a wonderful feeling that everything is possible. On an impulse, I turn to Ah Zhao and say, "Today is the happiest day of my life. I'm going to write it in my notebook and remember it forever."

Prime Minister's Son

After the Qing Ming Festival, everything seems to change. With the help of Baba's influential friends, Gege is admitted to the prestigious National University of Bian Liang. He spends his time attending classes, studying for the Imperial Examination and advancing his career.

At the university, he makes a new friend. Cai You 蔡攸 is eight years older than Gege and gifted in music. He teaches Gege to sing, compose songs and play the *qin*, a zither consisting of a wood frame and seven strings of twisted silk. Gege asks me for help in writing the lyrics. I do so gladly because a song is really a poem set to music, and I love writing poetry. I'm thrilled to hear my words being sung loudly, by my brother, for everyone to hear.

Gege shows Cai You my lyrics and he's delighted. Cai's father, the newly appointed Prime Minister Cai Jing 蔡京,

persuades Emperor Huizong to create a special *Da Cheng Yue Fu* 大晟樂府 (Bureau of Music of Great Brilliance). It includes a *Wan Qin Lo* 萬琴樓 (Pavilion of Ten Thousand Zithers) and is staffed by one *Da Si Yue* 大司樂 (Musician-in-Chief), two *Dian Yue* 典樂 (Music Managers), one *Da Yue Ling* 大樂令 (Music Officer), four *Xie Lu Lang* 協律朗 (Composers) and two hundred performers and dancers.

Huizong announces that Confucius and He both believe that *Ya Yue* 雅樂 (Proper Music) is beneficial and nurturing, whereas *Yin Yue* 淫樂 (Improper and Licentious Music) is corrupting and destructive. When asked the definition of Proper Music, His Majesty replies that *Ya Yue* consists of two kinds of music written and produced at the Bureau of Music of Great Brilliance: heavy and solemn music, or light and entertaining music. The former is to be performed at sacrificial rites and other official Confucian ceremonies, whereas the latter may be played during dinner parties, banquets and other informal gatherings.

Some time later, Huizong receives an unexpected fan letter from a distant land. Apparently, Emperor Yejong of the Korean Court of Goryeo has heard of the Chinese Emperor's growing reputation as a patron of the arts. After expressing his admiration, the Korean Emperor begs Huizong for guidance in the purchase of musical instruments from China. Filled with pride and gratification, Huizong immediately orders dozens of zithers, horns, flutes, cymbals, chimes and bells to be sent to Yejong as a goodwill gesture. Not long afterward, Huizong follows with an even larger gift of four hundred and twenty-eight musical instruments.

Since Gege is increasingly preoccupied with his studies

and classmates from the university, Ah Zhao and I are left more and more to our own devices. We talk for hours about nothing and everything—painting, sculptures, rocks, ghosts, history, family intrigue, court gossip or Ah Wang's bossiness. But mostly we talk about the meaning of art.

Ah Zhao believes that the goal of a great artist is to strive for artistic Truth, not just to make things look realistic. He thinks loving art will improve a person's quality of life—any person's life.

"An artist," he says, "is in touch with Heaven. In fact, he's an instrument of Heaven. Look at the trees, flowers, shrubs and rocks around us. How orderly Nature is! I feel that the source of our sense of beauty comes from Nature. A true artist is engaged in a spiritual quest. He's searching for his private Heaven."

One afternoon, Gege returns home from classes earlier than usual and comes into the playroom carrying a thick roll of silk. He plonks it down on the table and says to Ah Zhao, "There you are!"

"That's a long piece of silk!" I exclaim.

"Just over one and a half *zhang* long."

"It looks narrow," Ah Zhao says. "What's its width?"

"You *told* me to get as long and narrow a piece of silk as possible for our painting. This is only seven and a half *cun* wide."

"Length and width are perfect!" Ah Zhao replies. "The color is great too. Not too yellow. Not too white. Somewhere in between."

"What are you going to do with it?" I ask, full of curiosity.

"Remember the day the three of us were together on the

bank of the river at Qing Ming?" Gege says. "Ah Zhao promised to help me paint the view of the capital from the Longevity Gardens."

"It's going to be a magnificent picture!" Ah Zhao's eyes are shining. "Unlike any painting before. I have a vision of the Bian River meandering down the entire length of this long, narrow scroll. We'll sketch the boats and bridges on the water . . ."

"Will you include the *Hong Qiao* (Rainbow Bridge) with everyone watching the boat that almost capsized?" I ask.

"Of course we will! We'll also put in the farms, country roads, trees, people, animals and buildings along the shore. Exactly the way it was that day," says Gege.

"In the market I saw shops selling wine, grain, vegetables, cookware, lanterns, musical instruments, jewellery and all sorts of other goods. Don't forget to draw all the different people milling around: the farmhands, camel-drivers, goatherds, pig-farmers, as well as city folk such as peddlers, jugglers, beggars, monks, carpenters, scribes and fortune-tellers." I feel more and more excited at the idea of the picture.

"The main thing is to capture everything the way it was that day. How everyone dressed and walked must be faithfully portrayed. We'll draw the people, animals, buildings and boats accurately and represent every image in the correct proportion," Ah Zhao proclaims.

"What about the wheelbarrows, sedan chairs and carriages?" Gege asks.

"Put them all in!" Ah Zhao answers grandly.

"Won't the painting take months, if not years, to finish?"

"Probably, but so what? A great work of art is worth any

101

amount of effort and time. Done properly, this painting may even live on after we're all dead and gone." He looks at Gege's expression and reassures him, "No worries, my friend. I'll help you finish it if it's the last thing I do . . . I promise!"

"Let's start now!" Gege cries.

"There's no better time than now," Ah Zhao agrees.

"How do we begin?"

"I've got it all planned out. I have a stack of paper here. Each sheet is ten *cun* long and ten *cun* wide. And here's a pair of scissors. Let's begin by cutting the papers down to the same width as our roll of silk. Seven and a half *cun*. Now we unroll the silk and find out how many pieces of paper we need to represent the entire painting. Will you help us, Little Sister?"

We unroll the silk scroll, place the paper on top and count the number of sheets that cover its length. The answer is sixteen. Or, to be exact, fifteen and four-fifths, just shy of sixteen.

Ah Zhao rolls up the scroll and puts it away in his big wooden storage box by the wall. The boys begin to work in earnest. After various rough drafts on numerous sheets of paper, they decide to make the arched bridge the central focus of their picture. Next, they sketch the river meandering down the entire length from right to left.

"Think back on that day," Ah Zhao urges. "What did we first see when we came out of our gate?"

"A rural scene of crop fields, tall trees, narrow muddy lanes with donkeys, camels and oxcarts plodding along, and peasants plowing their farms with the help of water buffaloes," Gege answers.

"Very good," Ah Zhao says. "Let's depict the first part of our journey on this sheet of paper and label it 'One.' Remember, everything in proportion! Meanwhile, Little Sister, you can help us by writing down in your notebook everything you saw that day. Start from the moment we passed through our gate at home, and continue on as we approached the city. . . ."

We are so absorbed in our tasks that we don't hear Nai Ma coming into the playroom until she's standing immediately inside the door and calling loudly: "Little Sister! Your *niang* is looking for you! She wants to see you in her room right now."

Reluctantly, I put away my ink brush and notebook. Nai Ma is clearly anxious, and she whispers that Niang is in a very bad mood.

I must have done something wrong, but for once I can't think what it might be. The boys wish me luck.

I tidy myself hastily before knocking on Niang's door.

"Good evening, Niang."

Niang's eyes wander over me with open disdain, and I know she doesn't like what she sees.

"How unkempt you look!" she begins. "I think you're getting uglier and uglier as you grow older and taller."

Her unkind remarks make me wince. I try to answer, but I suspect a trap—one wrong answer and she'll strike. So I say nothing.

"Where were you just now?"

"I was in the playroom, helping Gege with his painting."

She sits down, and I can't help noticing that the turquoise silk of her robe goes perfectly with the pink cushions on her chair. Nothing is allowed to clash in Niang's rooms. The only thing out of place is me.

"Was Ah Zhao there also?"

"Yes."

"Did your father tell you we're on the verge of signing a marriage contract for you?"

I'm shocked and don't know what to say. Surely Baba would have told me if there was anyone seriously asking to marry me?

"No, Niang," I reply.

"He probably doesn't want to bring bad luck and ruin it by mentioning it to you—it has taken long enough to get to this point," Niang says. "This is what I want to speak to you about. You're growing up. While marriage negotiations are under way, you're not to spend too much time in servants' quarters or talking to them in a familiar way."

I can't think what she means.

Niang eyes me coolly. "Don't try looking innocent—you know the boy I mean. Your *baba* has a soft spot for him, and I must admit he is strangely talented for such a creature. If your *gege* likes to spend time with him, that's his affair, but I don't want any chances of a good marriage being ruined because you can't keep away from low company. Do you hear? What were you doing in Ah Zhao's shed anyway?"

I feel anger welling up inside, but try to control myself. "I already told you! Ah Zhao and I were both helping Gege with his painting."

Niang's beautiful face distorts with anger. "How dare you speak to me in that tone of voice? Just because your father dotes on you, you think you can do anything you want. When you're married, you'll soon find out things will be different. I hear your future mother-in-law rules her home with an iron hand. Even her husband, Commissioner Ye, is frightened of her. Let alone her son!"

Suddenly I'm not angry anymore but terribly frightened. Commissioner Ye's son is about forty years old, almost the same age as Baba. Besides being old, he's also known to have a terrible skin condition that leaves him with weeping sores all over his body, including his face.

"Please, Niang, please don't make me marry him—anybody but him. I'm sorry I was rude—just let me wait a few years before I get married. I'm not ready yet." I can hear the note of panic in my voice and know I'm humiliating myself, but I don't care.

Niang can't help smiling. "Oh—so now it's 'Please, Niang' and 'I'm sorry, Niang.' Well, it's too late, I'm afraid. For once you won't get your own way with your father—he needs this marriage to advance his career. When Commissioner Ye becomes the *Hu Bu Shang Shu* 戶 部 尚 書 (Minister of Revenue), your *baba* will be promoted to *Cang Bu Lang Zhong* 倉 部 朗 中 (Director of the Granary Bureau)."

A wave of anger hits me. "My mother would never have let me marry a man like that," I say bravely. "She would have protected me."

Niang laughs harshly. "You should count yourself lucky if he does choose to marry you. The Ye family is one of the richest in Bian Liang. Don't forget that most husbands want a pretty bride who is skilled in the art of pleasing men. Not only are you strong-willed and bad-tempered, you're not exactly good-looking or submissive, to put it bluntly."

"All the more reason you should let me stay the way I am. Besides, I don't want to get married. Don't my wishes count for something?"

"Frankly," she says with a cruel smile, "your wishes count for nothing. I'm warning you not to be too familiar with that Ah Zhao anymore. You're no longer a child but a young woman of marriageable age. The reputation of the entire Zhang family is at stake. So are your chances of making a good marriage. If your *baba* ever finds out you are bringing dishonor to his name by being too friendly with a servant boy, he will send him away—perhaps even throw him in prison. Now go and tell your brother to come to my room. I want to talk to him."

Baba's Birthday Party

I hesitate for a long time before daring to visit Ah Zhao the next day. Finally, I decide to wait until Gege comes home from university. From my window, I watch Gege enter the gate and dismount his horse, then I dash down to our playroom to see what Ah Zhao is doing. I find him hunched over a sheet of paper with brush in hand, deep in concentration. Almost immediately, Gege saunters in with an oblong-shaped red cardboard box.

"Oh, Little Sister! You're here too. Didn't Niang talk to you yesterday about your upcoming marriage?"

Ah Zhao looks up with a startled expression, but says nothing. I see he has outlined on paper the half-moon shape of the Rainbow Bridge, with a big boat approaching from the right.

I make a face at Gege. "Yes—what about it?"

Gege frowns. "You seem to be spending a lot of time in here nowadays. I'm sure Ah Zhao has better things to do than talk to little girls."

Ah Zhao remains silent as I stare at Gege, hardly able to believe my ears. "Oh sorry, *Niang*—for a minute I thought you were my brother, Gege, but now that I hear you speak I see it's you. Or is your name *Ah Wang*, the spy?"

Gege looks uncomfortable for a second, then laughs.

"Never mind," he says. "I have something to show you both—look at this!"

Running down the middle of the red box is a two-inch strip of gold paper inscribed with beautiful calligraphy.

"What's inside?" Ah Zhao asks.

"It contains an invitation to Baba's fortieth birthday party. Baba commissioned Teacher Lai to write his invitations for him, and it took him five whole days to complete them. I brought this one to show you before Little Chen delivers them. Impressive, isn't it?"

"Who is it addressed to?" Ah Zhao asks.

"Let me see." Gege scrutinizes the characters. "It says 'General Tong Guan, Bureau of Military Affairs, Military Advisory Office.' "

"Tong Guan?" Ah Zhao and I exclaim in unison.

"Wasn't he the eunuch who came here and gave me the letter from the Emperor?" Ah Zhao asks. "Has he been promoted to military general?"

"It sure seems like it! 'General Tong Guan,' it says here," Gege replies, studying the invitation.

"Isn't a eunuch a servant in the Emperor's Palace?" I ask. "How can a servant turn into a general all of a sudden?"

"Anything is possible. It all depends on the Emperor. What the Emperor wants, the Emperor gets," Gege says.

"How do boys become eunuchs in the first place?" I ask.

"They get castrated," Gege answers tersely.

"What's castration?"

"Don't you know anything? Castration means you get your *san bao* 三 寶 (three treasures: three male organs consisting of penis and two testicles) cut off so you're no longer a man."

"Isn't that what the farmers do to their bulls? Nai Ma once told me that after bulls get their male organs cut off they become obedient and mild-tempered. Only then can they be trained to pull carts or work in the fields. Not before."

"Nai Ma is correct. But eunuchs get to be servants in an Emperor's Palace, instead of pulling carts and working in the fields."

"Why would any boy want to become a eunuch?"

"The Emperor employs only eunuchs to serve his wife and concubines, so there are obvious advantages. . . ."

"Like what?"

"Eunuchs are with the Emperor and His women day and night. Being close to the seat of power, they become powerful themselves. That's probably how Tong Guan became a military general."

"Enough about eunuchs! Let's see the rest of the invitation," Ah Zhao says.

Gege opens the red box and shows us the booklet inside. On the cover page is Baba's name, as host, followed by seven more pages of elegant handwritten notes. Since Ah Zhao can't read, I read the contents to him.

The invitation begins by saying that Baba will be preparing a modest meal of fifteen courses at his humble home during the sundown hour on the Eleventh Day of the Seventh Moon. A list of the guests' names appears, together with their titles and accomplishments. This is followed by a description of the menu and the program of celebration. It ends by saying that Baba and his guests are looking forward to exchanging new ideas on art, calligraphy, music and poetry with the recipient during the forthcoming celebration of his fortieth birthday.

Gege looks at the guest list.

"These men are all Baba's most successful friends, and many have high positions in the government. Baba pointed some of them out to me when he took me to watch Emperor Huizong's coronation ceremony four years ago."

"What about their wives and children? Are they invited?" I ask.

"Of course not! Women don't count. Their names aren't even mentioned on the invitations."

"What about you, Gege?"

"Baba says I am still too young. My friend Cai You isn't invited either. However, the party will be held in the courtyard, unless it rains. So we'll have a perfect view from the window in my room."

On the day of the banquet, the house is full of delicious cooking smells. Everyone is busy preparing for the feast. When it's time, Baba dispatches his house servants to position themselves on the road and greet everyone with a personal card of welcome.

All the men arrive wearing official hats and handsome silk robes, mostly red, green and blue. One elderly man is clothed in a purple silk gown. He carries a walking stick and looks very distinguished, with his full head of gray hair and luxurious flowing beard.

Gege and I peek from the upstairs window of his bedroom as they alight from their carriages. Gege whispers that the elderly man is Cai You's father, Cai Jing, the Prime Minister.

"Why is he the only one wearing purple?" I ask. "The other guests are wearing red, blue and green robes."

"Only the highest grade of mandarin officials are entitled to wear the color purple. Prime Minister Cai Jing outranks everyone else here tonight."

"What about the other colors?"

"Different colored robes indicate a separate status. After purple comes red, then green. The lowest grade of mandarin officials wears blue."

"How long has this been going on?"

"Ever since the Tang Dynasty, four hundred years ago. The first Tang Emperor decided on the colors worn by the different ranks of mandarin officials. The Song Emperors followed this custom when they conquered the Empire."

"I see Cai Jing has attached a lift to his shoes, to make himself taller."

"Look at the cap on his head—the stiffened bamboo strip on each side can be bent straight, crossed or curved. Cai Jing wears his with the bamboo straight. This again shows he's of the highest rank."

The servants have placed a large square table and

padded bamboo stools in the courtyard. Hundreds of flickering lanterns line the walkways and cast a magic glow over the flowering trees and banquet settings. Baba comes out in a red robe to greet his guests. Hands clasped within his loose flowing sleeves, he bows slightly to each visitor while raising and lowering his hands and muttering "*Qing, qing*" 請, 請 (please, please) over and over.

He now takes a stool with both hands and places it in the position of honor, facing south in front of the table. The stool is spotlessly clean, but he brushes off imaginary dust with his hands and invites his guest of honor, Prime Minister Cai Jing, to sit. The Prime Minister duly lifts a stool of his own, dusts it off in a similar fashion and places it opposite himself, for Baba. All the other visitors are then seated around the table, according to rank and age.

Baba places a bowl of rice wine on a silver tray, holds it with both hands, faces south and pours the wine on the ground as an offering to his dead ancestors. He returns to the table, bows to Cai Jing and offers him the second bowl of wine, which Cai accepts with both hands.

Ah Wang and his helpers bring out more ewers of wine. Each ewer is cradled by a delicate, lotus-shaped porcelain bowl filled with hot water to keep the wine warm. The servants follow Baba and place a pair of chopsticks and a bowl of wine on a plate in front of each guest. Everyone rises to his feet, bows to Baba, wishes him a happy birthday and takes a sip of wine.

A beautiful woman dressed in a green silk blouse and pale blue skirt enters and plays the lute while the men are eating and drinking. She's a professional entertainer, hired for the occasion, and I have never seen her before. Her hair is elaborately coiffed into a tall bun with pins and combs shaped like butterflies and flowers. Her face is heavily made up with powder and rouge. Throughout the meal, this musician is the only female in the room, among all the men.

There's a knock at our door and Nai Ma brings us each a bowl of fried rice for dinner.

"Come, Young Master, it's not enough to watch others eat. You must eat too," she says. But we're too interested in the scene below to eat. When Nai Ma tries to insist, Gege shoos her away.

In the courtyard garden, the dishes are being served one by one: five kinds of dumplings (each with a different filling), roasted piglet, seasoned duck eggs, sautéed shrimp, goose liver, crab rolls, deer tongue, frogs' legs with beans, bear's paw, pickled vegetables, onion and vinegar chicken, bean curd with rice, steamed carp, quail soup and long life noodles. At the end of the meal, Ah Wang brings bowls of hot tea and individual little dishes of fresh fruit: grapes, sugarcane, jujubes (Chinese blackthorns), pomegranates, crab apples, red oranges, melons, pears and plums. After dessert, he clears the table. The men sit around and begin to converse in earnest.

Baba calls for a long scroll of paper, writing brushes, inksticks, water bowls and ink-stones. Everyone rolls up his voluminous sleeves as Baba grinds the ink-stick with water to make fresh ink.

"Look at Prime Minister Cai Jing's hands!" Gege whispers to me. "The nails on his little fingers are at least three *cun* long! They're all curled up!"

"How disgusting! It must've been years since he cut them! Why is he so lazy?"

"He's not lazy. He keeps them long like that to show the world how privileged he is. No manual labor for him, that's for sure! He uses his hands only for writing."

"What are they doing, Gege?"

"They're going to practice the *san jue* 三 絕 (three perfections) together: painting, calligraphy and poetry. Each will create an image or a verse to match and bedazzle the rest. Shhh! Quiet now! I want to hear what they're saying."

"I hear His Majesty wants to encourage the arts," says a balding, middle-aged man with a heavy beard and mustache.

"That's Vice Director Liang of the Ministry of Personnel," Gege whispers, and I marvel at his remembering all their names and positions.

"They say His Majesty aspires to be a latter-day sage-king, like King Yu the Great of the Xia Dynasty, three thousand years ago," Baba says with reverence.

"His Majesty is interested in many projects," an elderly man with a long sparse beard and high, squeaky voice replies. Gege nudges me excitedly and reminds me that I've seen him before. He's the famous Tong Guan, part Palace eunuch, part military general.

"Tell us more," Commissioner Ye says eagerly to Tong Guan. "You are the only one who lives in the Palace with His Majesty, therefore you probably know the most about Him."

"His Majesty will soon create a special Advisory Office to make changes," Tong Guan announces.

"What changes?" Baba asks.

"His Majesty intends to establish schools throughout the country to give more children an education, so they can compete in the Imperial Examinations. He also wishes to build public hospitals and cemeteries for the poor."

"How will He pay for all these benefits?"

"His Majesty will impose a special tax on salt and on tea. Any merchant selling salt or tea will have to pay this tax."

"Great changes!" Baba says approvingly.

"His Majesty was only seventeen when He came to the throne four years ago," Tong Guan says. "At that time I was already forty-six years old, having served first the Sixth and then the Seventh Emperor in the Palace before they died. The Eighth Emperor is entirely different from His father and older brother. Being a younger son, He never expected to be Emperor, so he learned to paint from an early age. He loves music, calligraphy, painting and poetry and has a passion for rocks. He recently founded China's first *Han Lin Hua Yuan* 翰林畫院 (Royal Academy of Art) and plans to make drawing one of the compulsory tests for the Imperial Examination. He says painting and writing have different names but possess the same body. I predict that, under His reign, artists will play a major role in the government."

"Is it true that His Majesty is planning to build a grand pleasure park full of precious rocks and rare plants?" Commissioner Ye asks.

"His Majesty loves rocks, especially odd-shaped ones," Tong Guan replies. "He has commissioned the famous architect Li Jie 李誡 to design a special garden to be named Genyue 艮嶽. The centerpiece of this new garden will be an artificial hill the height of twenty men. A waterfall will cascade down the mountain and drain into a pool full of rare stones, goldfish, geese and ducks. Monkeys and deer will roam freely among the trees and flowers."

"We need to recruit as many talented artisans as possible to help create the Emperor's vision," Liang remarks.

"What about that barbarian boy-sculptor of yours?" Tong Guan says to Baba suddenly. "The one who carved that jade dog for His Majesty's birthday. Is he still working for you?"

"Yes, he is."

"What's his name again? I've forgotten."

"He used to call himself Li, based on his father's barbarian birth name, Levy. You may remember His Majesty granting him the use of the imperial surname, so nowadays we call him Ah Zhao."

"He might be a suitable candidate for you," Tong Guan says to Liang.

"Would you mind if I hired him away from you, to work in my Ministry of Personnel?" Liang asks Baba.

"It's entirely up to Ah Zhao ... He's young and his whole life is ahead of him. He's free to consider offers and make his own decisions for his future."

"Does he have any relatives? Parents? Siblings? Wife?" Liang asks.

"No one. The boy is an orphan."

"Does he like working with rocks?"

"There's nothing he enjoys better than hacking into a mountain with hammer and chisel. I'm constantly being surprised by his prowess. He's capable of cutting, carving and polishing the hardest granite or jade into sculptures of the utmost beauty and poetic suggestion."

"Well, let's take a look at the boy now," Liang says to Baba. "Artisans who know how to work with rocks are hard to find."

Baba claps his hands to send for Ah Zhao.

Gege looks at me with a sober expression. "This meeting may change Ah Zhao's future," he says. "I hope he doesn't mess it up."

"Ah Zhao always knows what to say," I retort, and my stomach ties itself in a knot at the thought of Ah Zhao leaving us.

Ah Zhao enters the courtyard behind Ah Wang with his head bowed and his shoulders bent. He falls to his knees in front of Baba and touches his head to the ground three times.

"Old Master Zhang!" he says. "How lucky I am! I was begging Ah Wang for a chance to see you. He refused, but to my surprise, you sent for me! Thank you."

"Why did you want to see me?" Baba asks.

"I wanted to express my gratitude to you for the many kindnesses you have shown me. Your two precious children commissioned me to do a painting of a dragon for your birthday. I spent many months trying to render the image of a fantastic beast onto paper, but finally I gave up on the dragon. Instead, I decided on this simple sketch of a dragon-shaped rock painted on silk, which I now present to you. I hope it will please you."

He kowtows again before presenting a small oblong box

he is holding in both hands. Baba opens the box and takes out a silk painting rolled into a scroll, twice as long as it is wide. As he lays down Ah Zhao's birthday gift and slowly unrolls it, a collective gasp escapes the lips of the men round the table.

Instead of the frightening beast he has been painting, Ah Zhao has drawn a single black rock. We are too far away to see the image in detail, but it must be amazing because all of Baba's friends are speechless with admiration. They clap their hands in spontaneous applause. Many call for wine, to drink a toast to the young artist. They point out to one another the rock's jagged profile jutting proudly against the brown silk background; the perforations in the stone captured by many ink washes, patiently applied, tone on tone; the subtle patterns of the rock's dark and light surfaces; and the sprig of hardy green leaves sprouting delicately from the hollows.

"Did you give this painting a name?" Baba finally asks.

"Your worthless servant was thinking of calling it *Dragon Rock*," Ah Zhao replies, still kneeling.

"Excellent name!" Commissioner Ye says. "I see you have left space for an inscription on the left side of the rock. Why don't you stand up, come to the table and write a dedication to Magistrate Zhang. We'll help you compose a suitable verse."

"I am illiterate, Your Honor," Ah Zhao says humbly.

"I know His Majesty's likes and dislikes," Tong Guan suddenly interrupts. "I think He will be very impressed by this painting. I suggest I take it with me when I go back to the Palace tonight. In the morning, I'll ask His Majesty to write a few words in His distinctive *shou jin* 瘦金 (slender

A detail from *Qing Ming Shang He Tu* 清明上河圖 (*Along the River at Qing Ming*). This particular scene of the boat about to capsize is described on pages 64–65. The entire painting is seventeen and a half feet long and only ten inches high. Known as China's *Mona Lisa* and painted with ink on silk, it captures the holiday atmosphere of ordinary people celebrating Qing Ming, presenting a panorama of Song Dynasty life. Note the period clothing, hairstyles, headgear, sedan chairs, stalls packed with merchandise and the variety of boats on the river.

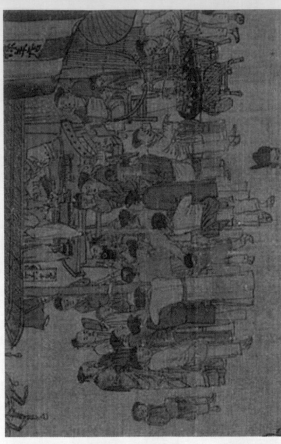

From the same painting, this detail shows the ornate guardhouse above the city gate described on pages 74–76. Some guardhouses also served as drum and bell towers. In ancient times, there were no mechanical clocks. Officials kept time by sundials, water clocks, sand clocks or by burning incense sticks. The public would be notified of the time by the daily beating of drums and bells at regular intervals.

A man with the sleeves of his jacket tied round his waist (front center) stands among a crowd gathered round an animated storyteller who has a luxurious beard and mustache. (This scene is described on page 178.) Storytellers have a long tradition in China. They combined classical history with contemporary humor to entertain the audience.

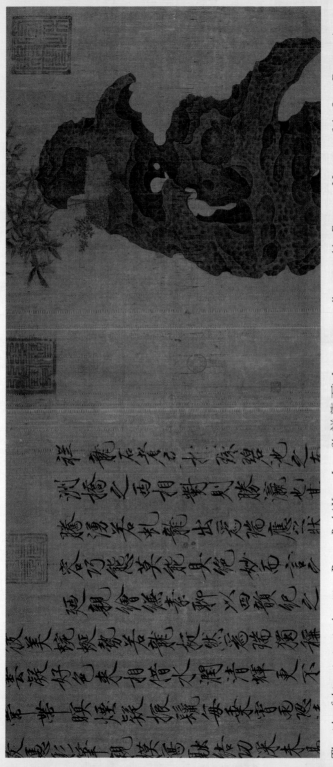

The title of this painting is *Auspicious Dragon Rock* (*Xiang Long Shi* 祥龍石). It was supposedly painted by Emperor Huizong of the Song Dynasty (see pages 118–119 and 128–131), whose *shou jin* 瘦金 (slender gold) calligraphy can be seen to the left of the rock.

吟徵調高窺下桐
松間疑有入松風
仰窺低審含情客
以聽無絃一弄中
臣京謹題

聽琴圖

The painting *Ting Qin Tu* 聽琴圖 (*Listening to Zither Music*) was also presumably painted by Emperor Huizong. It shows the Emperor sitting under a tree and playing the zither to two ministers and a young female attendant. On pages 152–153 Zhang Ze Duan tells his sister Zhang Mei Lan that he painted the attendant to look just like her, thereby making her famous and immortal. The calligraphy and poetry above the picture was written by Cai Jing 蔡京, the Prime Minister under Emperor Huizong.

gold calligraphy). That would really make this painting famous and immortal!"

"Will you do that for me?" Baba asks, his eyes shining.

"Of course!" Tong Guan says. "One more question, Ah Zhao. Did this painting come from your imagination or were you inspired by a particular rock?"

"Your Honor, I came across this particular stone lying by itself in the ravine at the back of my master's house one year ago. I thought it was special, and would visit it from time to time. It seems to be related to the earth from which it sprang and yet it stands alone. By painting it, I meant to release its spirit and set it free. I'm so glad everyone likes my painting."

"Why do you like rocks?" Liang asks.

"Rocks are full of meaning, don't you think? They are direct links to the essence of who we are. I love to work on pieces of stone with hammer and chisel. When I tap on a rock, I hear an echo and it reminds me of who I am."

Liang nods his head, and I know he is impressed, as is everyone else.

"You may go now, Ah Zhao," Baba says after a while. "Thank you for your birthday gift. You have done a wonderful painting. I like it very much."

"One more thing before you go," Tong Guan adds. "How big is this piece of rock on which your painting is based?"

"It's big. About *ba chi* 八尺 (over eight feet) tall and *liu chi* 六尺 (over six feet) wide."

"Can the rock be delivered to His Majesty's garden?" asks Tong Guan.

"Surely you are joking!" Baba answers. "A rock that size

will require at least a dozen men to move from my place to the Palace."

"Let me confide something," Tong Guan says. "At this very moment, His Majesty is having a special cargo ship built to carry an enormous boulder from *Tai Hu* 太湖 (Tai Lake) in the south to His Palace here. The Taoist priest Lin Ling Su 林靈素, His Majesty's spiritual advisor, has convinced Him that this particular rock is full of divine significance, and His Majesty has decided He must have it. Unfortunately, because of the rock's size, we might have to tear down some bridges and enlarge a few canals to bring it here. Compared to that, transporting your rock poses next to no problem."

"Where will these rocks be placed?" Commissioner Ye asks.

"In the enormous Genyue Imperial Pleasure Park, just outside the walls of His Majesty's Palace, which I spoke of earlier. Besides scholars' rocks and exotic plants collected throughout the Empire, the park will also have elephants, lions, leopards, rhinoceroses and a host of rare birds such as herons and tufted ducks. Presently, as many as thirty ships have been dispatched to every place under Heaven to transport the specimens to Genyue."

After Ah Zhao leaves, the men go back to their conversation. Gege listens intently to every word, but I'm tired; it has been a very long evening. So when Nai Ma comes and tells me it's time for bed I'm quite happy to go.

Dragon Rock Painting

Ah Wang keeps Ah Zhao even busier than usual after Baba's birthday party, assigning him the revolting job of emptying the latrines every morning. It's as if he's trying to punish him for being the center of attention at the banquet. The stench is so overwhelming that Ah Zhao stuffs his nostrils with dried jujubes to hide the noxious odor whenever he steps into the outhouse. Gege is also increasingly preoccupied, spending more and more time at the university, preparing for his impending Imperial Examination.

This gives me a chance to write a poem that I've been thinking of for some time. It's about the nature of friendship.

For years now, I've found it impossible to write in my bedroom, the room I share with Nai Ma. She means well, but she's always asking questions or engaging me in conversation when I don't feel like talking. Normally, I would escape to Ah Zhao's shed. Since Niang's recent warning, however, I don't dare go there so often, especially when Gege is not with me.

Fortunately, I have a secret hideaway that nobody knows about. It's the alcove part of the main parlor, hidden behind a latticed screen. This is where Niang and I listened to the monk who spoke about my foot-binding, years ago. Compact and well lit, it's furnished with a redwood table and comfortable chairs. When I want to be alone, I go there and can write undisturbed for hours on end. It's my very own private "writer's retreat."

Immediately after breakfast this morning, I sneak into the alcove when nobody is looking. I take my writing materials out of the cabinet by the wall, where I've hidden them behind Niang's best porcelain: ink in a flask, brush and paper. I arrange them carefully on the table, moisten my brush and begin my poem:

> *When we talk, there is always something new*
> *Our topics are endless and inexhaustible*
> *A poet's pen has turned this affinity to shape*
> *And given it a name. It is called*

As I concentrate on finding the next word, a man's voice booms out loudly somewhere in the same room: "I bring you auspicious news and inauspicious news. Which do you want to hear first?"

The voice is so close I almost jump out of my chair. Then I remember where I am. Keeping as still as possible,

I peek through the screen and see Baba entering the parlor behind a tall man with military bearing. Tong Guan! I should have recognized that voice as soon as I heard it.

I know I should declare my presence, but I'm embarrassed. Suddenly it's too late. I know that if I appear now, my *baba* will be shamed by having a daughter who hides and listens to other people's private conversations. My only alternative is to remain hidden and hope I'm not discovered.

"Auspicious news first, as befits my optimistic nature," Baba says.

"His Majesty thinks so highly of your *Dragon Rock* painting that He has already written an inscription with His own hand, in the space to the left of the image."

"Excellent! What's the inauspicious news?"

"His Majesty wants to buy the painting from you."

"Buy it from me? For how much?"

"As much as you like . . . or as little as you like . . . His Majesty instructed me to bring you one hundred ounces of silver as a starting price."

"A hundred ounces of silver for one painting by my barbarian servant!? And you consider this inauspicious news?"

"If I were you, I would give the painting to His Majesty as a present, and return His silver. In the long run, it's much more valuable to have His Majesty in your debt than to have a hundred ounces of silver. However, I say this as a friend. The decision is yours and yours alone."

"My thanks to you, General Tong. If that's what you recommend, that's what I'll do. But I still consider these to be good tidings."

"I haven't finished yet. In addition to the painting, His Majesty wants to buy the rock on which the painting is based. Is it still lying in the ravine at the back of your house?"

"I haven't yet seen the rock. Ah Zhao will know where it is. My barbarian servant is the only one here with a passion for rocks."

"His Majesty happens to share the boy's passion. For another hundred ounces of silver, He wants the Dragon Rock to be moved to the Palace garden as soon as it can be arranged; preferably today."

"That's why you brought the wagon and the guards! You came prepared."

"Yes, I did. I now need to tell you His Majesty's third and final request."

"Auspicious or inauspicious?"

"You be the judge. Along with that painting and the rock itself, His Majesty wants Ah Zhao to enter the Palace and be one of His artists-in-residence."

Baba is silent for so long that Tong Guan gets up from his chair and takes a stroll around the room before sitting down again. Meanwhile, behind the screen, I'm trying not to make a sound, but the thought of Ah Zhao leaving us is like a blow to my heart.

"You know the boy is an orphan . . . ," Baba finally says.

"So I've been told, but having no family just makes it easier."

"Makes what easier?"

"To subject himself to castration and become a eunuch."

"I was afraid of that," Baba says. "Is there any way that Ah Zhao can work in the Palace without castration?"

"That's out of the question."

"Then I must say no on his behalf."

"Are you saying no to His Majesty? Need I warn you of the consequences?" Tong Guan sounds outraged. "I can't understand why you are against his becoming a eunuch. What an opportunity for a penniless orphan!"

"All I know is that I would never allow my son to be a eunuch."

"Your son is your son. He will pass the Imperial Examination and become a Han Lin scholar one day soon. His future is assured, and he will marry and give you many grandsons. How can you compare your son to an illiterate orphan destined to be a servant for the rest of his life?"

"Maybe you are right," Baba says. "The only one who can decide on that life is Ah Zhao himself."

"Well said! There's so much prejudice against eunuchs that is unjustified. But if you place yourself in Ah Zhao's shoes, how and where would you find this sort of opportunity again?" Tong Guan's voice cracks as he says this, and I suddenly recall that he is a eunuch himself.

"Of all the ministers who work for our sovereign, you are the one most qualified to talk to Ah Zhao about this offer. May I send for him and leave the two of you alone?"

"If you like," Tong Guan says with a smile. "I will try my best to give him the pros and cons, so he can make a rational decision."

"Please wait here while I tell someone to get him."

Behind the screen, my heart sinks as I realize I will be trapped in the alcove even longer. I don't know what the punishment is for eavesdropping on such an important conversation, but I'm sure it's harsh. To my dismay, I feel a sudden cramp creeping up my crooked toes, into my leg. I bend down to massage my muscles, and my shoulder brushes against the latticed screen. It sways back and forth dangerously. I lunge forward and just manage to save it from falling. I hold my breath in terror, certain that Tong Guan has seen or heard something.

Luckily, no one has noticed. I hear Baba coming into the room, followed closely by Ah Zhao. Tong Guan must have had his back to the screen the whole time, and seen nothing.

Peeking into the parlor, I see that this is a different Ah Zhao from five days ago. Instead of his long, dark blue gown, he's wearing his everyday work-shirt and rough trousers. His hands are soiled from working in the garden. A pair of pruning shears protrudes from his breast pocket, and he smiles as he strides in with the exuberance of youth and high spirits.

"Old Master Zhang, you called!"

"Yes, Ah Zhao. I want to introduce you again to General Tong Guan, whom you met here five days ago at my birthday party. There's no need to kneel. You may remain standing. The General wants to have a private talk with you."

"I am honored," Ah Zhao says, smiling.

"How long have you been living at my house?"

"Close to four years."

"Have you been happy here?"

"You have treated me like a second son. I am happy and content."

"You are a very talented young man," Baba continues.

"I regret that I did not ask Teacher Lai to teach you reading and writing when I first took you in. Now others are beginning to recognize your abilities. General Tong here wishes to make you an interesting proposition. You are more than welcome to stay and work here for the rest of your life, but you should listen to other opportunities when they arise, and decide for yourself. I will now leave you alone with the General."

Baba leaves the room. At first there's an awkward silence as Ah Zhao and Tong Guan smile at one another. Finally, General Tong signals Ah Zhao to sit on the chair previously occupied by Baba.

"I gather you're an orphan," Tong Guan begins.

"Yes, I am."

"Would it interest you to know that I too am an orphan?"

"So we are two of a kind," Ah Zhao says.

"I know only too well how it feels to belong nowhere; to be in perpetual exile. In your case, it's probably worse because I can see from your wavy hair and blue eyes that you are not even a Han Chinese."

"Yes. I am a barbarian. As such, I will always be a *wai ren* (outsider)."

"I myself was passed from relative to relative," Tong Guan says. "Then, when I was nine years old, a distant cousin 'sold' me to an old eunuch at the Palace and I became his adopted son. Two years later, my foster father persuaded me to undergo the operation and I became a eunuch also, just like him. From that time until now, I have served in the Palace continuously for over thirty-nine years."

Ah Zhao leaned forward. "Forgive me for asking, but are you happy? Do you have any regrets?"

"As soon as I entered the Palace, I knew I had found my permanent home. Strange as it seems, things came together for me when I became a eunuch. Yes! I am happy. I am also immensely successful. There's no way I could have become who I am today without having entered the Palace."

"It's certainly a great honor for me to see you today," Ah Zhao says.

"I showed His Majesty your *Dragon Rock* painting after I returned from your master's birthday party . . ." Tong Guan hesitates at this point.

"Did He like it?" Ah Zhao asks eagerly.

"His Majesty is a great patron of the arts. He has a general interest in chess, music, dancing, poetry, calligraphy, antiques, architecture and gardening, but He's passionate about only two subjects: rocks and painting. And those two passions happen to be combined in this painting of yours titled *Dragon Rock*."

"How lucky I am!"

"His Majesty is in the process of creating two new departments in His Imperial Palace. The first is a Royal Academy of Art. He's currently modernizing the Civil Service Imperial Examination so that candidates will be required to come into the Palace and be evaluated on their paintings, under the eye of the Emperor himself."

"Why is His Majesty so interested in painting?"

"The Emperor believes that beauty is virtue. He intends His reign to be remembered for its culture. However, since you cannot even read or write, you will obviously not be part of the Royal Academy."

"I understand, General."

128

"The second unit will be called *Rui Si Dian* 睿思 殿 (Palace of Divine Inspiration). It will be staffed entirely by eunuchs of talent. I'm happy to say that His Majesty has just appointed me to be the Director of this division."

"Congratulations!"

"His Majesty and I both feel that you will be an ideal candidate for this second unit."

"I don't understand . . ."

"Then let me illustrate by showing you your own painting; your birthday present to Magistrate Zhang."

Tong Guan removes the silk scroll from a box at his side and unrolls it.

Ah Zhao is clearly surprised when he sees that ten vertical lines of characters have been written to the left of the rock.

"Who wrote all those words?"

"What a shame you can't read! Otherwise you'd know at once who has written them."

"I had deliberately left the space blank for my master to write a poem . . ."

"Well, the painting's new master has chosen to write something there instead."

"Who is that?"

Tong Guan laughs. "You have no idea of your own luck, do you?"

"Am I lucky?"

"You are the luckiest man of all under Heaven because His Majesty has taken ownership of this painting."

"Is Magistrate Zhang aware that His Majesty has taken ownership?"

"I informed him just now."

"What did he say?"

"What *can* he say? He's happy for you. I must say, though, you don't seem as pleased as you ought to be."

"I'm still trying to understand. Everything is happening so fast."

"Do you know what the Emperor wrote?"

Ah Zhao shakes his head. "Please read the words to me."

"*Xiang Long Shi* 祥龍石 (*Auspicious Dragon Rock*). His Majesty begins with these three words because they represent the title of this painting."

"What else has His Majesty written on my painting?"

"Ah Zhao, I must tell you that this is no longer your painting. It's vital to remember this at all times."

"What do you mean?"

"I just told you that His Majesty has taken ownership of this painting."

"I know that. But nothing can change the fact that I painted it."

"His Majesty is the *Tian Zi* 天子 (Son of Heaven). As such, He can change anything. Let me read you what He wrote in the fifth vertical line: *nai qin hui jian su liao yi si yun ji zhi* 廼親繪縑素聊以四韻紀之. Here, His Majesty is saying that He personally painted this on silk and is commemorating it with the four lines of rhyming poetry which follow."

"But He didn't paint it. I did!" Ah Zhao sounds outraged.

"Curb your tongue! Don't you realize you can be

beheaded for claiming this? How dare you contradict the Emperor! Do you want to lose your life?"

"Of course not."

"It may very well come to that, if you're not careful. See here?" Tong Guan points to the painting. "In the fourth line of the poem, His Majesty wrote *gu feng cai bi qin mo xie* 故 馮 彩 筆 親 模 寫 (therefore, using a colored brush, I copied the rock myself). He then wrote the words *yu zhi yu hua bing shu* 御 製 御 畫 並 書 (Imperially produced, Imperially painted and scripted). It ends with His signature written in cipher, *Tian Xia Yi Ren* 天 下 一 人 (First Man of All Under Heaven). That's the autograph of His Majesty, followed by the impression of His seal."

"So, His Majesty has claimed authorship as well as ownership of my painting."

"You should be flattered—it means your future is assured. His Majesty is in the midst of recruiting China's best and brightest artists to paint for Him. They will be housed in a special new building named the Palace of Divine Inspiration. It will be part of His imperial compound. He wants to offer you a position there at the starting salary of one hundred and ten ounces of silver a year."

"One hundred and ten ounces! I can hardly believe my ears! What do I have to do for this fabulous salary?"

"You are to spend your time painting. However, you will not choose your own images to paint; His Majesty will choose them. You will no longer work as an individual, and must leave no trace of yourself on any of your works."

"Whose name will be on the paintings?"

"His Majesty's name."

"How many artists will be working in this Palace?"

"The exact number has not been determined yet. Besides artists, we are also recruiting writers, calligraphers, poets, engravers and sculptors. There will be a few hundred eunuchs altogether."

"Eunuchs! Did you say eunuchs?"

"Yes. I said eunuchs."

"Does that mean I'm to become a eunuch?"

"Yes, of course. Only eunuchs are allowed to live and work in His Majesty's Palace."

"I'm afraid I will have to decline."

"Don't be so hasty! His Majesty is offering you a once-in-a-lifetime opportunity. If you take this road, you are bound to become rich and successful. I can guarantee this."

"How so?"

"Being the Son of Heaven, the Emperor is all-powerful. Everyone under Heaven dreams of being close to His Majesty. You are one of the few whom He has noticed, and whose work He admires. Once you enter the Palace, you can exert more and more influence, just like I did."

"Is there any possibility that I can work for His Majesty without becoming a eunuch?"

"No."

"Will I be able to travel?"

"Only if His Majesty allows you to do so. Presently, His vision for you is to stay in the Palace of Divine Inspiration and paint whatever He wants you to paint."

"I understand. May I think this over before making my decision?"

"The Palace of Divine Inspiration will be completed in

two months—you can have until then. His Majesty is giving you a lot of face by recruiting you. Do not disappoint
Him. Otherwise, the consequences may not be pleasant for
you or the Zhang family. Is that clear?"

"Perfectly clear."

"I hope it is clear, for your sake. Remember, His Majesty
is not used to being denied. Meanwhile, please show me
where the rock is so my men can cart it to the Palace."

Through the screen, I watch them leave. With a huge sigh
of relief, I try to get up, but my legs are numb from being
still for so long. Just as I am shaking them to get the cir-
culation back, I see a hand coming round the side of the
screen. My heart gives a giant lurch as the screen is pushed
to one side.

"I knew it must be you," Ah Zhao says, and my stomach
returns to its usual place. "I saw the screen move when I
first came into the room! Did you know the edge of your
dress was sticking out nearly the whole time I was talking
to Tong Guan? What on earth are you doing here, Little
Sister?"

I try to get up, but collapse in an undignified heap on the
floor because one of my legs is still asleep.

"It's a long story. What are *you* doing here? I thought
you were supposed to be showing the General where the
rock is."

Ah Zhao points to his gardening shears.

"I left these so I would have an excuse to come back. I'll
catch up with the General now, then I must speak to your
Baba. He's the only man I trust to give me sound advice.
Come on, I'd better give you a hand up before I go."

Ah Zhao's hand is warm in mine, and I wish I could feel its support there all the time.

"We must talk this over, Ah Zhao. You can't go to live in the Palace—it will destroy you."

Ah Zhao gently releases my hand and picks up his shears.

"Don't worry, Little Sister. It may not come to that. I have to go now."

Marble Snail

During the next two months, Gege's friend Cai You spends more and more time at our home. After classes on most afternoons, the two sit in the garden next to Ah Zhao's shed and practice the zither for hours on end. They keep asking me for new lyrics, which I gladly supply. I find that I really enjoy writing words to songs. It's much easier than learning to play the music. Besides, I like to hear my lines being chanted loudly, over and over, for everyone to hear.

Baba comes home earlier than usual today, and finds them playing the zither and practicing one of my lyrics. He joins us at the garden table and tells Ah Zhao to bring out the best tea in the house, as befits the son of the Prime Minister.

"Good tea!" Cai You exclaims, sniffing the fragrance.

"Glad you like it," Baba replies. "This particular tea was picked from the bushes in our private tea-garden, in early spring. At that time of the year, the tea-bushes are covered with silvery-white leaves, tender and fragrant, that resemble needles. We compress the leaves into tea-cakes and dry them in the sun. When guests like you honor us with your presence, we cut off a bit of cake and grind it with a mortar and pestle. Then we pour freshly boiled water over the powder. We call this 'white tea,' because of its color."

"I've never had tea as delicious as this!" Cai You says. "May I present some of this tea to His Majesty as a special present from you? The Emperor is a great connoisseur of tea and is presently writing a book titled *Da Guan Cha Lun* 大觀茶論 (*Treatise on Tea*)."

"I will be honored to do so. Please tell His Majesty that the quality of the water is as important as that of the tea." Baba beams. "The water in this tea isn't drawn from the well in our courtyard but carried from a fresh spring one *li* away. All the utensils used are reserved for making tea and nothing else. A knife that cuts shrimp or garlic is never used to cut tea-cakes in my kitchen! The tea-cake knife cuts only tea-cakes."

"I've noticed how tranquil and beautiful your garden is," Cai You says, pointing to the door as Ah Zhao walks into his shed. "Look at the bamboo framing the door of this simple wooden hut with its thatched roof! Every trunk is as high and round as the next. And the asymmetry of the paving stones along this path leading to the main house. How did you achieve this poetic effect? Who designed it?"

There's a short silence as Baba looks around at his garden proudly, with fresh eyes. "Well, I suppose my head servant, Ah Wang, has a lot to do with it . . . ," he replies vaguely.

"Oh, Baba!" I interrupt impatiently. "You know very well it's Ah Zhao who's the brains behind it!"

Cai You makes the kind of face people make if they step in dog poo.

"Ah Zhao!? The barbarian garden boy who just served us our tea? Surely you're joking? Most barbarians can't even read or write, let alone design something as sublime as this garden! They're barely human!"

I'm furious, but also shocked, as it has given me a glimpse of how other people might see Ah Zhao.

"He's not just the garden boy, is he, Gege?" I wait for Gege to defend him, but he has gone red and is trying to pretend he hasn't heard.

This just makes me angrier. "He's our friend, isn't he, Gege?"

Cai You gives a silly little laugh. "Your friend . . . the garden boy . . . is this true, Ze Duan?"

Gege mumbles something that could have been a yes, but says nothing else. To make matters worse, I know that Ah Zhao can hear everything from his shed.

Fortunately, Baba explains to Cai You that Ah Zhao is a very talented artist, and part of our household, rather than just a servant. Cai You gives another silly titter and says he admires Baba's commitment to the arts.

I've had more than enough, so I make my excuses and go to my room. After a while, Nai Ma comes in and says that Cai You has gone home. I go looking for Ah Zhao, so I can apologize, but finding him is not as easy as I'd hoped. Finally, I find him near the ravine at the back of our garden, pruning the dead branches off a pine tree growing out of a rock. I can tell he wishes that each branch he is lopping off is Cai You's head. I've never seen garden shears look more dangerous.

"Come on, Ah Zhao," I say to him. "Don't listen to that idiot Cai You—he's just not worth getting upset about."

Crack—another dead branch hits the ground. Ah Zhao picks it up and breaks it over his knee.

"It's not just him—everyone thinks the same thing. No matter how well I paint, I'll always be the barbarian who is barely human. An outsider, in exile for the rest of my life. Even to your brother!"

I feel desperate to make Ah Zhao realize how important he is to us. "You have no idea of your effect on others, Ah Zhao. When Gege and I are with you, everything comes alive. I know he didn't behave too well back there . . . goodness knows what came over him . . . but in his heart he's perfectly aware of your perception and intelligence. Surely you know we both think you're a genius?"

"A genius!? What are you talking about?"

"Remember the time you, Gege and I came to explore this ravine for the first time, and saw this very tree growing out of rock? You made us tap out hunks of granite that day with hammer and chisel, to make paving stones for the path in the garden. Afterward, you did a painting of the gnarled tree so beautifully that its branches appear to be twisting in the wind every time I look at the picture. As for the little snail you carved out of the small piece of black granite that broke off, I like it so much that I've slept with it under my pillow every night since you gave it to me."

Suddenly Ah Zhao is not angry anymore.

"Have you really?" he asks, visibly moved.

"Yes—and I often look at it and wonder what you were thinking when you carved it."

"I remember very clearly. When I first came across that small, broken piece of granite, its shape appealed to me. It was just a stone, but it had a touching quality. For some reason, it reminded me of you."

I smile. "Maybe it's because I tend to hide behind my books. It takes courage to be a writer—especially a woman writer. The act of writing seems so final. Once you've put your thoughts down on paper, you can never take them back."

"For whatever reason, I saw within that stone the image of a little girl too shy to show her talents, just as a snail is afraid to show its horns. I worked on that piece of rock, and something precious emerged. That snail used to be part of a ravine, but now expresses a young girl's hidden dreams . . ."

"From now on, every time I look at my snail, I'll think of you extracting a living symbol from a cold mountain," I reply. "And now my dream is that Tong Guan will forget all about you, and you'll stay here with us forever."

Ah Zhao suddenly looks into my face. "Don't you realize that change happens all the time? Nothing is forever. Everyone knows that your *niang* is trying to arrange a marriage for you. Do you honestly think you'll be living here much longer yourself? With a bit of luck, you'll marry a rich man, bear lots of children and live happily ever after."

"No!" I cry. "I'll never marry. I'm going to be a writer."

"Only time will tell what is to be your destiny," he says sadly. "But one thing's for certain. Unfortunately, I don't think Tong Guan will forget about me."

Decision

Sure enough, a letter arrives for Ah Zhao two months later. Baba reads it to him. Of course it's from Tong Guan, and in it he demands the presence of Ah Zhao at the Palace of Divine Inspiration, within ten days.

Gege and I walk over to Ah Zhao's hut and wait for him. The two of us sit on the planks covered with bamboo matting that he uses as his bed. I look around the room as Gege rests his arms and head on the tree-trunk table.

"This room has hardly any furniture, but I love it," I tell Gege. "To me, it's the most beautiful room in our entire house."

"Why do you think we like it so much?"

"As soon as you step inside the door, you know you're in a special place. This room belongs to someone who has no money but possesses the good taste that money can't buy.

Look at the bare earthen floor, the bamboo-covered benches, the thatched roof, the mud walls mixed with straw, the curved wooden pillar, the unevenly spaced bookshelves, the windows cut on several levels. What does it remind *you* of?"

"It reminds me of an ink-wash painting: simple but elegant. I know what you mean, Little Sister. Whenever I come here, I feel that time is suspended. Even though I know we're living during the reign of the Eighth Emperor of the Song Dynasty, this room could have been here during the Tang Dynasty or even one thousand years ago, during the Han Dynasty. It would have looked exactly the same. Sometimes, I see Ah Zhao as a prophet, a figure of light, or a character out of myth. At other times, I see him as a man of destiny. . . ."

"What's the phrase he likes to say that makes you feel so good?"

"*You he bu ke* (is anything impossible)?"

At this moment, the door opens and Ah Zhao walks in, looking white-faced and exhausted. He flops down on the bamboo mat next to Gege and says nothing for quite a while.

"I'd hoped this day would never come!" he finally mutters, and puts his hands over his eyes as if he doesn't want to see what's in front of him.

"We all did," Gege answers impatiently. "What does Baba advise you to do with the Emperor's offer?"

"Before I answer that question, I need to clear my brain first. Tell me, my friends, what is the meaning of art? Why is art important?"

"That's a big question," Gege says. "But I'll tell you this, Ah Zhao—you are one of a kind: a true artist. You strive for Truth every time you touch a brush. The rest of us are not like that. We merely strive for resemblance. We may be good at copying flowers and birds, but there's no depth and no substance to our drawings."

"You flatter me, my friend."

"Gege's right," I say. "Art is important because it gives meaning to life. Since Heaven is the source of Order, a great artist like you is searching for Truth, for Order and for Heaven in your work."

"To be an artist, then, is to improve life and give it meaning. If that's the case, how can I subject myself to becoming a eunuch in His Majesty's Palace? For a salary of one hundred and ten ounces of silver a year, they want to rob me of my manhood and my art."

"How can the Emperor claim your painting to be His work without even asking you for permission? That's simply not right," I say indignantly.

Gege sighs. "It's more complicated than that, Little Sister. The great thing is that His Majesty is prepared to give money to support the arts. What's more important—a work of art, or the artist who painted it? Great works of art continue to be appreciated long after the artist has died. Some people would even claim that without the Emperor's support, many paintings wouldn't have been created in the first place. So in a roundabout way, these works were really the Emperor's creations, even though He didn't paint them."

I want to shake Gege. "Aren't you confusing the word 'creation' with the word 'possession?'"

"Well, there are many ways of looking at art. It all depends on your personal point of view. . . ."

143

Ah Zhao gets up impatiently. "I hate to interrupt your philosophizing, Gege, but I need to make a decision. General Tong Guan wants me to live in the Palace of Divine Inspiration with hundreds of other eunuchs and paint pretty pictures at His Majesty's command for the rest of my life. During the first two years, he says I'll be placed on night duty and become a *dai zhao* 待詔 (imperial attendant)."

"Night duty?"

"Yes! Apparently, His Majesty always keeps a painter on night duty; a versatile painter who is adept at painting anything: flowers or birds or stones. The Emperor gives frequent dinner parties during which He might suddenly summon for a painting. The imperial attendant needs to be ready to produce a painting at all times."

"Are you going to accept the job?" Gege asks.

"I would rather die than live in that Palace and become that type of a painter. Nothing could be worse than living with hundreds of eunuchs, painting thousands of pretty pictures all signed by the one name, Huizong. I need to figure out a way to disappear without involving you two or your family."

"Not involve us!" Gege cries. "Nothing of the sort! We *want* to help you!"

"I told your Baba about my conversation with Tong Guan. He advised me to leave the capital and hide, if I have no intention of ever entering the Palace. Turning down an offer from His Majesty will not be viewed in a positive light."

Gege's face betrays his sadness, but I realize with sudden insight that he's prepared for this to happen. In a way, he *wants* it to happen.

"I'll never be able to find another friend like you," Gege says. "I feel it in my bones. You must know that both my sister and I admire and love you. No one can ever replace you in our hearts."

Ah Zhao puts his arm round Gege's shoulder. "You have your whole life ahead of you. Every boy our age wishes he could be in your shoes. When I'm gone, you're bound to make other friends. Soon enough, you'll pass the Imperial Examination and become a brilliant minister in His Majesty's court. I have no doubt."

"Where will you go?" Gege asks. "What about money? Do you have any?"

Suddenly he jumps up.

"Wait here, both of you   I'll be back in a moment."

As Gege runs from the shed, Ah Zhao turns to me. "Well, Little Sister, it has come to this."

I'm overwhelmed by grief. "You have no idea," I say, my voice choking with despair, "how bad I feel right now. Please, please won't you take me with you? Unlike Gege, I have no future. I would do anything to come with you."

"If only I could! But how would we live? You know as well as I do that nothing can be more hopeless. Besides, you're only thirteen years old!"

"I could take the jewelry my mother left me," I say.

"I wish I had your courage and confidence, Little Sister," he says sadly. "But honestly, where would we go? With my height and barbarian features, they'd catch us in no time. If you run away with me, your *baba* would never forgive me; he'd think I've betrayed him, and accuse me of ruining you. I can't do that to him. He's my benefactor."

"But will I ever see you again?" To my embarrassment,

I start to cry. "I long to go off somewhere and be free; have a room of my own, just like this shed; create an oasis where I can write. . . ."

"Perhaps I can help you do that, one day. The three of us have had such happy times, especially when we were working together, with Gege and me painting and you writing. . . ."

"Will you come back for me when you're rich and famous?" I plead desperately.

"My chances of that aren't great!" he says sadly. "But I promise I'll come back to see you, one day."

"When?"

Ah Zhao thinks it over before he answers soberly. "Whatever happens, I'll wait for you at our ravine, on or before the Qing Ming Festival, in three years' time. By then, you'll be sixteen and I'll have an inkling of what my life is going to be like. Right now, I feel as helpless as you. I wish we were free to do what we want; be happy together with no Baba or Niang to worry about. But they are around, and we're not free."

"Everyone under Heaven knows what my *niang* has planned for me."

"You have shown yourself to be stronger than your *niang*, once before—you can do it again, if you have to. Be brave! I have faith in you."

There's the sound of running footsteps, and Gege bursts through the door.

"You'll need money," he manages to say, between breaths. "I have some saved. You must take it all."

I can see that Ah Zhao is touched. "Thank you, my friend," he says. "One day I hope I'll be in a position to pay you back. Your *baba* has also given me all the silver from Tong Guan, as a farewell gift, so I'm well set up."

"What else can we do?" Gege asks.

"You've done more than enough already. You two are the only family I have, and this shed my only home. But it's only a home because of you. Wherever I go, I'll always carry the memory of you in my heart. I give you my solemn promise that I'll be back."

We help Ah Zhao pack his few clothes into a bag, together with his paintbrushes, cash and silver ingots.

"No more tears, Little Sister!" he says to me. "I'm afraid life is often unfair. Make your right hand into a fist and wrap your left hand round it. Gege will wrap his hands round yours, and I'll wrap mine round his. There! Now we have a giant fist, let's make a pact that we'll always be united in our hearts and minds, wherever we may be."

His eyes are glinting with tears as he picks up his bag and strides away. He closes the door gently behind him, but opens it again almost immediately.

"Nearly forgot!" he exclaims. He runs to the wooden storage box, by the wall, where he keeps his art supplies, lifts the lid and stuffs a thick roll of silk and some paper sketches into his bag.

"Don't look so sad!" he says. "Remember that one single positive dream is more important than a thousand negative realities. Since we're young and free to create whatever we wish, *you he bu ke* (is anything impossible)?"

And then he's gone.

Two Gifts

Next day, Baba sends Ah Wang and Little Chen to report to Tong Guan that Ah Zhao has run away in the middle of the night. For a while, Baba is fearful that the Eunuch General will blame him for Ah Zhao's disappearance, or, worse still, will launch a search for the young fugitive. At their next social gathering, however, Tong Guan says nothing when his friend Cai Jing asks Baba about Ah Zhao.

"Barbarians don't think like normal people," Commissioner Ye remarks, after Baba tells everyone of Ah Zhao's disappearance. "I'm sure your servant has no idea what a great opportunity General Tong Guan was giving him. He'll remain poor all his life and be buried in a pauper's grave. That will be the end of him."

Since Tong Guan is sitting there, Baba does not mention that Ah Zhao had shown no hesitation whatsoever in rejecting a eunuch's life of power and luxury in favor of freedom and liberty.

Every hour of every day, I feel I'm about to hear from Ah Zhao, but there's only silence. Baba allows Gege and me to keep his hut in the garden, but after a while I'm the only one who goes there. Gege takes the final part of his Imperial Examination and passes, amid much celebration.

Baba is practically bursting with pride, especially on the day of *Dong Zhi* 冬 至 (the Winter Solstice Festival), when Gege and Cai You are chosen, along with Baba, to escort the Emperor in an important procession. They dress in formal robes and caps and proceed to *Tai Miao* 太 廟 (the Grand Ancestral Temple) to present offerings to Huizong's ancestors at the *Yuan Qiu* 圓 丘 (Round Mound Altar). The parade runs south from the *Xuan De Men* 宣 德 門 (Gate of Virtue Proclaimed) of the *Da Nei* 大 內 (Inner Palace) to the *Nan Xun Men* 南 薰 門 (Southern Infusion Gate) of the *Da Wai* 大 外 (Outer City) and is accompanied by seven elephants, fifty flag-holders, dozens of drummers and gong players as well as two hundred musicians and dancers dressed in colorful costumes. Tens of thousands of onlookers line the imperial main road to watch the parade, falling to their knees at the sight of His Majesty dressed regally in his imperial yellow robes.

After the ceremony, Huizong and his entourage return to the Palace, accompanied by processional music "loud enough to shake Heaven and Earth," according to Gege.

Then His Majesty proclaims an amnesty to hundreds of prisoners who are lined up in the courtyard. They are set free by the guards, while the Imperial Military Band plays wind and percussion instruments. Gege says he has Cai You to thank for being included in the Emperor's inner circle.

When Gege and Baba come home from the Palace that evening, our family sit together in the dining room, and eat our traditional *Dong Zhi* dinner—hot dumpling soup. These delicious dumplings look the same, but each has a different filling. Baba says that today, the day of the Winter Solstice, has the shortest daytime and longest nighttime of any day in the year. The name *Dong Zhi* means "winter has arrived." From tomorrow on, the days will get longer and longer until *Li Chun* 立春 (Spring Equinox), when daytime and nighttime will be of equal length. I ask Baba why and he says it's because of *Yin* and *Yang*. *Yin* is female and darkness whereas *Yang* is male and light. The two are not opposites but mirror images of one another. He promised to get a book from the market that will explain everything. The title of the book is *Zhou Bi Suan Jing* 周髀算經 (*Astronomy and Mathematics in Ancient China*). It was written fifteen hundred years ago and will teach me *Tian Wen* 天文 (the Language of Heaven).

Besides excelling in his studies and climbing the ladder of success at Huizong's court, Gege becomes increasingly active in the *Da Cheng Yue Fu* (Bureau of Music of Great Brilliance) where his friend Cai You has been appointed *Da Si Yue* (Musician-in-Chief). Gege continues to ask for my help in writing lyrics for Cai You to sing and perform for the Emperor. I give the songs titles such as "Flowing Water," "Mist and Clouds Over the River," "Wild Goose Lost," "Refrains of a Prisoner."

In the last song, I write:

> *Like a caged bird,*
> *I have wings but cannot fly.*
> *Like a horse in a forest,*
> *I have legs but cannot gallop.*

Gege complains that my words are too sad, but he and Cai You adapt my lyrics to their music anyway.

"Why do you ask for more when you criticize me all the time?"

"We're not criticizing," Gege protests. "We *love* your work. Cai You was saying just yesterday that your lyrics are extraordinary. They have such depth and insight. Some lines simply take one's breath away!"

"That's right," Cai You adds. "Your words make my music unforgettable!"

This makes me so happy I work even harder.

In return for Gege's helping him with his music, Cai You tries to advance Gege's painting career. He gives advice whenever he's here, which seems to be nearly every day, as far as I can see.

"I'll tell you the best way to get on, Ze Duan," says Cai You. "You should forget about yourself as an artist and give credit to His Majesty wherever possible."

"That should be easy enough!" Gege replies.

"In short, Gege, flattery will get you everywhere!" I say sarcastically.

I'm pleased that, despite his newfound importance, Gege can still blush.

In order to impress the Emperor still further, Gege combines art with music and paints a portrait of Huizong playing the zither under a tall pine tree in the garden of the Royal Academy. He names the painting *Ting Qin Tu* 聽琴 圖 (*Listening to Zither Music*), and presents it to His Majesty on His birthday. The Emperor is so pleased that he orders Prime Minister Cai Jing to write a few lines of poetry above the image, to commemorate the occasion.

"Should I mention that Your Majesty is the one playing the zither in this painting?" Cai Jing asks.

"Of course," Huizong answers, beaming.

"Who should I say is the artist?" Cai Jing asks.

There is a short silence. Then Gege says hastily, "His Majesty is the artist as well as the subject of this painting."

"Well said, Zhang Ze Duan!" Huizong comments, obviously pleased. "Do you know that the particular zither I'm shown playing in the picture was made three hundred years ago by the renowned Tang Dynasty instrument maker Lei Wei 雷威 (Mighty Thunder)? Lei Wei even gave that zither a name, *Chun Lei* 春雷 (Spring Thunder). Presently, my agents are searching far and wide for the best zithers in my Empire. My collection will be housed in the Pavilion of Ten Thousand Zithers. Although the total number of zithers will be vast, my favourite zither will always be Spring Thunder."

This story makes me laugh, especially since Gege says that he has sneaked my likeness into the painting. He drew me as a meek little maiden in a green robe standing next to a minister dressed in blue. Because there are only four people portrayed (Emperor, two ministers, girl) and I'm the only female, Gege says he has made me famous and immortal. But even as I'm laughing, I wish for the millionth time that Ah Zhao were here, to share the joke.

I also wish he could see the different suitors that seem to be coming out of nowhere for me, in spite of my big, ugly, unbound, natural feet. Besides Commissioner Ye's son, with the skin disease, the field has now widened to include the Prime Minister's son Cai You (but only as his concubine, since he already has a wife), General Tong Guan's nephew and many others.

I don't know whether Gege's success at court has anything to do with my rising popularity, but matchmakers are definitely beating a path to our door. Baba, Niang and Nai Ma talk to me endlessly about making a good match. Niang, in particular, is desperate to find someone who will take me off her hands.

I keep infuriating her by repeating that I don't want to marry—and that I especially don't want to marry the one with the skin disease, who persists in his suit. I feel quite powerful as I realize that no one can force me to marry if I don't want to. They plead, cajole, persuade and threaten in turn, but it's useless.

I've been reading about Buddhist nuns who become female poets. In the nunnery, these women spend their time studying, thinking and writing. Learning about these women's lives gives me the first glimmer of hope I've had since Ah Zhao went away.

Nai Ma says there's a nunnery adjacent to a Buddhist *Tie Ta* 鐵塔 (Iron Pagoda) near her village, just northeast of Bian Liang. Despite its name, the Iron Pagoda is made of brick, not iron. It has thirteen stories and is almost fourteen *zhang* tall. Inside is a spiral stone staircase, while the exterior is made of fifty different kinds of glazed brick with over one thousand five hundred carvings of Buddhas, monks, singers, dancers, lions and dragons.

When I ask my Baba about visiting the Iron Pagoda nunnery and becoming a nun, he thinks I'm joking, and tells me I won't get good noodles in a Buddhist convent. After I convince him I'm serious, he's furious and says that no daughter of his is going to shut herself away from all under Heaven. I suspect, however, that Niang is secretly on my side. I know I would be, if I were her.

After breakfast every morning, I go to Ah Zhao's shed and sit at his large round table. I make myself a pot of hot tea and read my books. Then I pour water on the ink-stone, grind the ink-stick and make fresh ink. I moisten my brush, open my notebook and write my lyrics, stories and poems.

Sometimes, I hold imaginary conversations with Ah Zhao. I whisper to him that I miss him . . . but when I try to put down on paper these thoughts that are not for the eyes of strangers, I'm unable to do so. At those moments, my heart is full of inexpressible emotions that are felt but unspoken. I tell myself that, if he were here with me, we would not need to talk at all. We could pretend we were children again and go rambling in the woods along the ravine, forgetting the woes and cares burdening our minds.

Nothing interests me except my books and my writing. I read and write all day, and sorrow vanishes when I use that magic. I find it incredibly consoling to be able to turn to this activity any time I wish. Writing is my source of recreation as well as my salvation. It gives me enormous pleasure to think of the many unwritten poems I have inside me. That's when I repeat to myself Ah Zhao's favorite phrase, "*You he bu ke* (is anything impossible)?"

As the third Qing Ming Festival approaches, I start counting the days with the help of my wonderful book *Zhou Bi Suan Jing* (*Astronomy and Mathematics in Ancient China*), which Baba bought for me at the market. By reading this book, I'm starting to understand the relationship between astronomy, mathematics and the calendar.

In my notebook I draw a calendar, beginning with Dong Zhi. The second new moon following this festival is New Year's Day. Fourteen days afterward is *Yuan Xiao Jie* 元宵節 (the Feast of Lanterns), when homes and shops throughout our city are ablaze with lamps.

Every morning, I make tea in Ah Zhao's shed and cross out another day on my calendar. Today is *Li Chun* (the Spring Equinox) and daytime is equal to nighttime. The term "*Li Chun*" means "spring is here." For the next two months, the days will get progressively longer and longer until the *Xia Zhi* 夏至 (Summer Solstice), which will have the longest day and shortest night of the year. Between the Summer Solstice and the Autumn Equinox, the days will gradually shorten. This continues until the arrival of the

Winter Solstice, when the cycle of *Yin* and *Yang* begins all over again.

Ah Wang is busy organizing the annual *Li Chun* Ceremony of the Plow for Baba's tenant-farmers. Since Baba is too busy to attend, Ah Wang dresses Gege in his official blue silk robe and cap, to take Baba's place. Blue is the color for entry-level mandarin officials such as Gege.

Accompanied by Ah Wang, Gege walks over to the farm next to our house where a new wooden plow, a water buffalo, and a crowd of colorfully dressed tenant-farmers are waiting, some carrying flowers. They have made a fake water buffalo out of a bamboo frame covered by five differently colored pieces of paper representing the *Wu Xing* (Five Elements):

Black for metal
White for water
Red for fire
Green for wood
Yellow for earth

Gege and Ah Wang lead the farmers in a parade from Baba's farm to the local Buddhist temple, where they burn the paper water buffalo. The altar is elegantly decorated with plum blossoms and five kinds of fruits. Everyone kneels and prays for a good harvest.

While Gege is telling me about his role in the Spring Equinox ceremony, all I can think of is my calendar. Fifteen more days and it will be Qing Ming. But there's still no sign of Ah Zhao. Will he come? Does he remember his promise? Didn't he say *"I'll wait for you at our ravine, on or before the Qing Ming Festival, in three years' time"*?

Most of Gege's days are spent at Huizong's various palaces, teaching students to paint and sign their work with the Emperor's name. Huizong holds frequent dinner parties for His ministers, friends and clansmen. Eager to display His talents in the Three Excellences—*shi, shu, hua* 詩, 書, 畫 (poetry, calligraphy and painting)—Huizong often entertains His guests by bestowing on them gifts of painting and calligraphy supposedly "done by His own hand." In reality, many of these works are drawn and written for Huizong by Gege and his students.

Meanwhile, in Huizong's Palace of Divine Inspiration, hundreds of talented eunuch-artists and calligraphers are at work producing thousands of images of birds, flowers and other small animals in the stilted style favored by the Emperor. These paintings are exquisite and decorative, but appear "empty" and devoid of feeling or personality.

I complain to Gege that the pictures look as though they've been mass-produced by a mechanical brush that has been taught to paint, but he's not in the mood to listen. He's often in a bad mood these days as, despite all his hard work and unquestioning support for the Emperor, he's unable to achieve his main ambition—which is to be *Han Lin Hua Yuan Shang Shu* 翰林畫院尚書 (Director of the Royal Academy of Art). He has started to visit me some evenings, in Ah Zhao's hut, since I'm the only one he can trust to complain to.

Tonight, Gege comes home earlier than usual because

the weather is bad. He enters Ah Zhao's shed without knocking and finds me sitting by myself in front of my notebook.

"Written any new lyrics lately?"

"No," I reply as I ask myself whether I dare to return to the ravine again tonight. I have visited it three times already: the first time early this morning, and then twice more after I crossed out today's date (Qing Ming) on my calendar. Each time, the ravine was deserted. But today is the last day for Ah Zhao to keep his promise.

Outside the rain is pouring down. I'm sorely tempted to take another look at the ravine, but worry that Ah Wang will report my odd behavior to Niang. I imagine him telling her that I've made a total of four trips by myself to the ravine today. The last visit in the midst of a thunderstorm. And in the dark, no less.

Better not risk it again. Instead, I heat water and make a pot of tea.

Gege and I sit side by side at the big round table, painting, writing and talking, the way it used to be with Ah Zhao.

"It's just not fair, Little Sister! I slave for years, learning the right way to do things and please everyone before myself. But I still can't get the one job I want more than anything in the world."

"Ah Zhao always said that life is not fair, but if I could give it to you it would be yours in the blink of an eye," I say. Despite himself, Gege laughs.

"It's something nobody can give me, Little Sister," he says. "To become Director, I need to create one distinctive painting. A painting that will elevate me above all the other artists without arousing the envy and resentment of the

Emperor. The trouble is that I've been trying to paint like everyone else for so long, my paintings have lost their *qi* (energy). I can only paint birds, trees and flowers that look exactly like everyone else's. I'm no longer able to stand out like *he li ji qun* 鶴立雞羣 (a crane among hens)."

"Actually," I say, "I'm not sure that you ever could."

Gege sighs. "No, you're probably right. I am a good copyist, which is why the Emperor likes me."

He looks down with disgust at the image of a white cat he just painted on a piece of silk.

"It's very pretty," I say.

"Come on, Little Sister—you don't have to pretend. I know you don't like it, and I know you think I've sold myself by allowing the Emperor to claim all my work. I'd only say this to you, but the Emperor is welcome to the credit for most of the rubbish I paint these days, anyway."

"Remember the dragon Ah Zhao painted for Baba's birthday?"

"Of course. What an impressive piece of work that was! Not like this awful cat here, produced and reproduced a thousand times over. Huizong has gathered the talents of His Empire and turned them all into little Huizongs to paint pictures and write calligraphy just like His."

"What happens to all these paintings?"

"He gives them away. It's customary for an Emperor to give presents to His guests at the end of an imperial feast. During last night's dinner at the Imperial Archives, Huizong gave each guest three hanging scrolls of painting and calligraphy. There were seventy-five ministers at the dinner, so He dispensed over two hundred paintings in one evening."

"Did the guests like them?"

"Like them? They were fighting among themselves to be first in line! Their hats were askew and their belts and pendants were all twisted and broken. The spectacle was quite undignified!"

"If Ah Zhao had accepted Tong Guan's offer, I suppose he would have become one of the anonymous painters in the Palace of Divine Inspiration, never to be heard of again."

"Those were the days, weren't they, when the three of us were growing up together and the future seemed limitless? Don't you wish we can be children again, the way we used to be?"

"I think of that time often. Yes! I wish we were children again. I'm scared of growing up,. . . Don't know how to grow up and don't want to. I wish I could feel the way I used to feel in those days. Full of hope and optimism! To be able to shout out to the world with conviction, *'You he bu ke?'* (Is anything impossible?)!"

"I can't help wondering—" Gege begins, when suddenly Nai Ma pushes open the door. She's dressed in the thick padded jacket and black hemp trousers she reserves for traveling. She's holding two oblong paper boxes and a dripping umbrella.

"So this is where you are!" she addresses me. "I've been looking everywhere for you."

"Where have *you* been in this horrible weather?" I ask.

"Little Chen comes from the same village as I do. Your Baba gave him permission to use the coach to go home and sweep his parents' grave today. Little Chen was kind enough to give me a ride, so I went to visit my sister."

"Oh of course—today is the Qing Ming Festival!" Gege exclaims. "I had forgotten."

"What's in the boxes?" I ask as Nai Ma opens her umbrella and sets it to drip on the porch.

"I'll come to that. Guess who was waiting when Little Chen drove back and turned into the road that leads to your Baba's mansion?"

"Tell us!" Gege says.

"It was Ah Zhao!"

When I hear his name, I feel a spasm in my throat.

"How is he?" I ask, trying to sound casual.

"He looked thin and tired."

"How did he know you were in the coach?" Gege asks.

"He didn't. He recognized the coach and stopped it. He was expecting to see your *baba,* and was surprised to see me instead."

"Why didn't he come in?" Gege asks.

"He didn't want to."

"What did he say?" I ask, feeling my heart flipflopping in my chest.

"He asked after the two of you. I told him of Gege's success at court. Then he asked whether you, Little Sister, were married and I said no."

"What is he doing?"

"He didn't tell me, only that life has not been easy. He has a present for each of you."

"A present!" Gege says. "So that's what you're carrying."

"Yes—Ah Zhao says each present comes with its own message, and you'll know what the message is. The heavier box is for you, Young Master."

Gege opens his box and takes out a long, narrow hand-scroll. He lays it on the table and gradually unrolls it from right to left. The magnificent panorama of the Bian riverbank slowly appears before our eyes. There it is again, exactly as it was on Qing Ming, three years ago: the fields, crop-farms and narrow country lanes just outside our home; the market stalls close to the city proper; the Rainbow Bridge thronged with spectators gawking at the vessel below; the colorful boats docked along both sides of the river; the splendid city gate with its awe-inspiring flying eaves; the hotels, temples, residences and mansions sparkling under the cloudless sky.

The three of us look with awe at the painting for what seems like an eternity. I'm back there again on that golden afternoon, eating noodles in the tea-house, admiring merchandise in the stalls, rambling along the shore among the trees and fields, wriggling my toes in the cool, clear water. Yes! Ah Zhao has captured everything! It's exactly the way it was "along the river at Qing Ming." Every time I think I've had enough, I notice something new to stir my imagination and need to look all over again.

"Do you know what message Ah Zhao is sending you?" Nai Ma suddenly asks.

"Yes, of course!" Gege says without hesitation, and I nod agreement.

"What? I don't get it." Nai Ma is puzzled.

"Ah Zhao has just given me what I want more than anything in the world: the Directorship of the Royal Academy of Art!"

"In this roll of silk?"

"Yes! All wrapped up in this roll of silk! Show Nai Ma the seal mark, Gege!" I exclaim.

Gege unrolls the scroll to the very end and points to the circular red chop mark bearing the name of the artist.

We see Gege's name staring back at us:

張 擇 端
(Zhang Ze Duan)

"Wah! This long scroll must have taken Ah Zhao at least a year to paint! And he puts *your* name on it! How generous!" Nai Ma is impressed. "I'm curious to see what Ah Zhao has given you, Little Sister!"

My hands are trembling as I prepare to open my present. On the lid of the box are three words, beautifully written in his distinctive calligraphy. No, not my name. The words are:

請 小 心
(Please be careful)

What is he saying? Why is he warning me to be careful? Is there a ghost hiding in the box? What will I find when I open it?

Inside is a black-and-white silk painting, much shorter than the other one and square-shaped. I unroll it and flatten it on the table, but I have trouble making out what I'm seeing. Gradually, the lines and shadows clarify themselves and I see the silhouette of Ah Zhao's prominent nose superimposed on my crippled foot.

"My old eyes can't understand this painting," Nai Ma complains. "It looks like a big ink blot that's out of focus."

"It's his self-portrait, isn't it?" Gege asks me shrewdly. "Big Nose!"

I shrug my shoulders and say nothing. I'm in turmoil. My heart is pounding and blood rushes to my temples. I hear a poem:

> *I'm Big Nose!*
> *Who are you?*
> *Are you Bad Foot?*
> *Then we're a pair.*
> *Don't say anything.*
> *They'll punish us*
> *For you being me*
> *And me being you.*

"In my humble opinion, Gege's Qing Ming painting is much prettier than this weird one!" Nai Ma pronounces as she positions my painting next to Gege's for comparison. "Look at the detail and fine lines in Gege's, with the people, boats, animals, buildings, vehicles, sedan chairs and trees all in perfect proportion! One wrong move with his brush and this entire scroll of ink-on-silk painting would have been ruined! No second chance! Now look at Little Sister's painting, where the ink appears to have been thrown onto the silk any old how! The only beautiful thing here is the calligraphy on the lid of the box! Even I can see that. Did Ah Zhao write these three characters himself, do you think?"

"Probably! Ah Zhao can do anything he sets his mind

to," Gege says, turning to me. "Nai Ma has a point, though, don't you think? The painting he gave you *does* look sort of strange. In fact, it looks unfinished. What's his message to you, Little Sister?"

"I'm asking myself the same question."

Flight

But of course I understood Ah Zhao's message. He couldn't have said it more clearly if he'd come in and announced it. However, a small voice inside warns me to guard the knowledge to myself. For once, I manage to keep quiet.

Perhaps it's the three words "Please be careful" that he wrote on the lid, as if there's something precious, fragile and breakable within the box; something to be treasured and protected at all cost.

The rest of the evening seems endless as I pretend that nothing has changed. Gege wants Nai Ma and me to keep on looking at his newly acquired painting, pointing out a thousand and one different details for us to admire. He repeats over and over how pleased the Emperor is going to be with him, as if he already believes the work to be his own.

After an interminable time, Nai Ma says she's exhausted, and retires for the night. Gege goes on and on praising his painting, even though I say hardly a word because I can't wait for him to leave.

When Gege finally goes to bed and I'm left alone at last, I sit and stare at Ah Zhao's gift to me.

"Am I right about your message?" I ask as I study his haunting profile overlaid on my broken toes. "Your painting makes me feel less alone," I tell him. "Are you saying we belong to one another?"

In one sense, Nai Ma and Gege are both correct: what a weird picture! But if you look at it from a different perspective, this double image becomes a pictorial metaphor, a symbol to express Ah Zhao's personal longing and dilemma.

It looks unfinished, Gege has said. Ah! That's because the friendship between Ah Zhao and me is not finished. The three words "It is finished!" will never be said of us.

Instead of *weird*, this picture is brilliant, original and profound, I tell Nai Ma silently. Ah Zhao is representing his perceptions by a radically different and unconventional method. He is expressing his feelings and fears, instead of merely copying what his eyes perceive at any particular moment. He has explored the corridors of his mind and juxtaposed the image of my crippled foot with the shadow of his face, combining our separate vulnerabilities within a single framework. Along with his gift is a warning and a query: "請 小 心 !" (Please be careful!) and "Are you prepared to face the world with me at your side?"

"You are a genius, Ah Zhao!" I say to his portrait.

Genius he may be, but I need to make some important decisions. Am I to run away with him tonight?

Outside, the rain continues to cascade down torrentially. I roll up the painting and put it back in its box with the three words "Please be careful" on its lid. Why is he warning me? Is he waiting for me right now, as promised? In the pouring rain?

"Whatever happens, I'll wait for you at our ravine, on or before the Qing Ming Festival, in three years' time."

That's what he said, three years ago, when he left. Does he remember?

Thin and tired. That's how Nai Ma described him. I long to see him, but I need to think a while longer. Why? For the same reason he wrote his message on the lid of the box: "Please be careful."

Why did he write those words? What is he saying? Am I to be careful because the consequences of our meeting will be momentous and irrevocable? Or is it the other way round? And he is warning me not to expect too much?

What he doesn't know yet is that my heart is tied to him as a boat is to its rudder. My childhood is over, and there's nothing here for me anymore. I'm prepared to pay any price to go wherever Ah Zhao wishes to take me.

The sounds of the household gradually die down as I creep back into my bedroom. Nai Ma is snoring loudly behind her curtain. Years of experience tell me that she won't wake. It feels strange to think that this might be the last time I'll be with her, but I have no regrets. She would like me to marry a rich man and bear children for her to look after. But she'll never approve of Ah Zhao as my husband, let alone accept him as her master.

Slowly and quietly, I pack some clothes and Ah Zhao's painting into a linen bag. I look at my books, regretfully . . . they're too heavy for me to carry. But I take my notebook, ink-stick and writing brushes.

The jewels left to me by my dead mama are concealed in a small silk pouch beneath a pile of clean underwear. I tie the pouch to my belt and make it part of my costume, underneath my padded silk-cotton cloak. Mama's legacy consists of two pairs of gold earrings, a fabulous pearl pendant, a gemstone bracelet, three jeweled combs and an imperial jade hairpin with a stem as thin as hair.

Before marrying Baba, my teenaged mama worked for two years as lady-in-waiting to a previous Emperor's favorite concubine at the Imperial Palace. Being a skillful seamstress, Mama designed and stitched a special dragon-and-phoenix pillow, out of kingfisher feathers, for the concubine's birthday one year. This pleased the consort so much that she and the Emperor ordered a Palace eunuch to bring out His Majesty's treasure chest. With His own hands, the Emperor personally selected two items and gave them to Mama as her wedding present. The first is the pendant with a large lustrous northern pearl, over one *cun* in circumference, said to be priceless. The other is the hairpin made of imperial jade. This jade is of such high quality that light appears to shine through its edges, creating an emerald-green translucence of incredible depth and beauty.

* * *

Outside my room, the house wraps me in its dark silence. I feel my way along the walls and creep downstairs toward the front door. Everything looks strange and frightening in the blackness, but I bite my lip and press on. In my mind, I've already left and this house is no longer my home.

The heavy wooden front door creaks loudly as I open it. I hold my breath, but no one comes. Rain is pelting down. I close the door softly behind me, open my umbrella and pick my way through the pitch-black wetness, toward the ravine at the back of the garden. It's so dark I can hardly see the path. In no time, my new cloth shoes are sodden. Nai Ma finished making these shoes only two days ago. Because my feet are still growing, she takes my footprint every few months. Painstakingly, she cuts pieces of cloth according to the latest tracing, glues five or six layers on top of one another and sews them together to make the sole. Then she measures the height of my crooked toes and cuts the silk so the top of the shoe will fit.

I sneak along, my shoes making ugly squishing noises with every step. Something small and quick darts furtively in front of me. It brushes my leg, then disappears. I'm so scared I almost fall. Is it a rat or a raccoon? I can't tell. I stand, paralyzed with fear. A fox howls, and an owl hoots in the eerie silence.

After a while, the rain slows and the air is still. A sliver of moon shakes free of its cloud-cover and casts a faint, silvery light over the flowerbeds, fish pond and stands of bamboo. I close my umbrella and step through the round opening in our garden wall. Now it's easier to see. I hurry along the rough, graveled path sloping down toward the

170

ravine; past the ghostly, moonlit pines and shrubs; past the big boulders and jagged terrain incised in craggy bedrock.

All this time, I've had no doubt that Ah Zhao will be waiting for me. But as I approach his favorite twisted pine tree, growing from a fissure in the weathered rock, I'm suddenly uncertain. "Am I dreaming?" I ask myself. "What am I doing here in the middle of the night? What if there's a wild tiger behind those bushes, waiting to pounce?"

I creep past a shrub and a sharp branch jabs my arm. I stumble and almost drop my bag. Before I have time to think, a voice in the darkness says, "*Qing xiao xin* (Please be careful)! Allow me to carry your bag!"

Ah Zhao emerges from the shadow. We stand and look at one another for a very long time . . . then we both begin to speak at once. This makes us laugh, and suddenly it's as if we've never been apart.

"You have no idea how often I've dreamed of today, all through these three years away from you!" Ah Zhao says. "It's a miracle that you've come to me like this!"

"Please be careful!" I say softly. "Those are the words you wrote on the lid of my box . . ."

"Yes," he answers simply. "That's my message to you . . . and you understood!"

His voice is full of love, and I wish I could keep this moment forever. . . . But he says, "Come, Little Sister, we must leave quickly. A friend is waiting for us with a carriage. He'll take us to the river, where there's a boat leaving at first light. When we're safely on board, then we'll be able to talk."

We make our way toward the back wall of Baba's property, at the far end of the ravine. I'm hurrying to keep up, but I stumble and slip on the wet grass and gravel. Finally, Ah Zhao stoops down and tells me to climb on. I sit astride his neck with my legs hanging over his shoulders, like a little girl, feeling protected and secure.

"My friend is waiting on the side lane, by the back wall. It's safer than the main carriageway."

"But how—"

"Don't worry, I'll help you over the wall."

"It's so high—"

Suddenly Ah Zhao stops.

"What is it?"

"Shhh! Listen! I can hear something."

We stand absolutely still, but all I hear is the sound of our breathing.

"You must have imagined it, Ah Zhao. . . ." But even as I speak I see something moving in the trees. Is it a deer or a bird?

Without a word, he sets off again, walking as fast as he can. I clutch onto his hair. He holds my bag in his left hand while steadying me with his right. In the distance, I see the garden wall and hear the horse chomping on the other side. If we can just get over the wall, I think, we will be safe.

At that moment, I hear footsteps and Ah Wang's voice shouting out to someone. Now I'm scared. Fear enters quickly, flooding the hollow spaces around my heart, making me tremble. Ah Zhao grasps my legs firmly and sprints for the wall.

The wall is very high. Ah Zhao lets me down and calls

out to his friend, who answers immediately. He throws my bag over to the other side. "Hurry!" shouts the friend. Ah Zhao scrambles up the wall as if it were a ladder, and I know I can't do this. The voices behind us are louder. A hopeless horror crawls up my leg from my crippled foot. I wonder if the terror will grow and grow until my brain blows apart under its relentless pressure.

Ah Zhao reaches down from the top of the wall and holds out his hand. Desperately, I try to grab it and clamber up, but it's too difficult. My foot keeps slipping and I can't hold on. The same weird feelings as before come flooding back. "Is this a nightmare?" I ask myself. "Am I dreaming or is this real? Will I escape, or will they catch me? What is my destiny?"

Even as my mind races, I struggle to find a foothold and reach the top. The rough rocks scrape my legs and hands. Unexpectedly, and all at once, Ah Zhao manages to catch both my arms as I jump upward, and he's half-pulling and half-lifting me up the wall. I make it to the top and lie there, catching my breath, while Ah Zhao jumps down the other side.

"Come now, Little Sister! Jump! I'll catch you!"

I feel a cramp creeping up my bad foot, and a fierce pain in my left shoulder. Something is horribly wrong. Can a person's arm be pulled out of her shoulder? I crawl on my right hand and knees and try to stand up. The pain is so excruciating I almost pass out. My left arm hangs uselessly at a grotesque angle. With a superhuman effort, I get to my feet and am just about to jump when I hear a familiar voice.

"Little Sister! Stop!"

There is only one person under Heaven who can make me hesitate at this moment.

"Gege! What are *you* doing here?"

"I'm here to stop you making the biggest mistake of your life! Don't jump! I forbid you!"

A wave of nausea hits me.

"You, of all people! Surely you understand?"

"I won't let you do this, Little Sister!"

"Why?" I ask, in agony.

"You will disgrace Baba and make our family the laughingstock of Bian Liang! I won't allow it! My decision is final!"

"Does Baba know?"

"Not yet! I haven't told him. Come home with me and I won't say anything to him, ever. It's our secret."

A pang goes through me when I hear him. How many times throughout our childhood have I heard him say this very sentence to me?

"How did you find out?"

"Oh, Little Sister! I knew as soon as I saw his gift to you. Did you really think I wouldn't recognize his message? He and I were like brothers. . . ."

"What about his gift to *you*?"

There's a short silence as he ponders my question. I see the shame on his face. His eyes look shifty in the moonlight.

"What about it?" Gege finally answers defiantly. "Nobody forced him to put *my* name on that painting. He did what *he* wanted to do. Besides, I was the one who conceived the idea for that painting to begin with!"

"So *you* created that painting all along! Oh, Gege!

I would give everything under Heaven to have you the way you used to be."

Suddenly I hear Ah Zhao's voice, urgent and harsh with anxiety. "Come, Little Sister! Jump! You must jump now!"

I take one last look at my brother and turn to jump. An agonizing pain shoots from my left shoulder, through my entire body. My foot twists on the uneven stones, and I hear myself screaming as I fall. . . .

Is Anything Impossible?

The voice on the wire recorder faded into silence, leaving the room strangely still and empty. CC leaned forward on her red recliner, her eyes fixed on the machine lying on Dr. Allen's desk. It was as if she was willing it to keep on talking, but there was nothing left to hear except the click click of the recorder whirring on.

CC tried to speak, but her throat felt closed and tight.

"That can't be all . . . what happened to them?"

Dr. Allen got up from his chair and switched off the machine.

"I'm sorry, CC. This was the last time Zhang Mei Lan spoke. It seems her connection with you began with your fall in the marketplace and ended when Mei Lan herself fell."

"But I need to know whether she managed to escape with Ah Zhao!"

"I wish I could give you all the answers, but we might have to be satisfied with curing your headaches and bad dreams. I think you feel a lot better than before your therapy, don't you?"

He seemed so determined for CC to feel better that she laughed. "Yes! Yes! Thank you, Dr. Allen. I haven't had a single headache since you began treating me with hypnosis. It really helps to understand why the Qing Ming painting looks so familiar. Before that, a mysterious feeling would come over me whenever I looked at that hand-scroll . . . like seeing a face I know well but not being able to remember her name, no matter how hard I try. But I still have one important question: how do I know so much about Zhang Mei Lan and Gege in the first place?"

Dr. Allen opened his desk drawer and took out the book that had fascinated CC for so long.

"I can only make an educated guess. What we know for sure is that the painting exists. It was painted in the time of Emperor Huizong, during the Song Dynasty. The artist was Zhang Ze Duan, who lived from AD 1085 to 1145. These are all historical facts that have been verified. However, you already knew that yourself from looking at this book so often."

"But the book doesn't say anything about Ah Zhao or Mei Lan. How can I tell you so much about them under hypnosis? Could I have been Mei Lan at one time?"

"There are a few possible explanations. For example, there's a thing called a 'false memory,' where people think they remember an event, but it's really an incident they've heard or read elsewhere. This can be triggered by trauma— such as your accident. But I have to say that the level of detail stored in your memory is extraordinary. Madame Wu and I have shown the transcript of this recording to a professor of history, and he recognized many of the people you mentioned."

"That doesn't make sense! How could I know their names under hypnosis without knowing them when I'm not under hypnosis?"

"Well . . . ," Dr. Allen began. Then he stopped and looked at Grandma Wu.

"Yes?" Grandma Wu prompted.

"Well, CC, as Madame Wu here keeps reminding me, there are many who might believe that you were remembering incidents from a life you led in the past."

Grandma Wu took the book from Dr. Allen and opened it at the painting of *Along the River at Qing Ming*. She traced one of the figures with her finger. "See this man here? He has taken off his jacket and tied the sleeves around his waist. That's something I do when the weather is either too hot or too cold and I can't make up my mind. Eight hundred years ago, Ah Zhao or Zhang Ze Duan saw a man doing this and captured his image on silk. In addition, look at this same man's posture: arms folded in front, shoulders thrust back, feet apart. That's my posture exactly! That's how I like to stand! Was this man my ancestor? Am I his descendant? Do I look like him? Who knows? If two people born eight hundred years apart can choose to carry their jackets and fold their arms while standing in exactly the same way, why can't you believe that CC was a young girl named Zhang Mei Lan during the Song Dynasty? Instead of inheriting Mei Lan's features, or the way she carries her jacket, CC inherited some of Mei Lan's memories. Why is that impossible? Many people, such as the Tibetans, believe in re-incarnation. At death, a person's essence doesn't vanish forever. It passes on to another. Just like a dying candle lighting a new one. Even if you don't believe that the Dalai Lama is the reincarnated God of Compassion, isn't rebirth a happier way of looking at death?"

"That makes a lot of sense," CC said. "But it means Mei Lan and Ah Zhao would have really lived at that time, as well as people such as Tong Guan, Cai Jing and Cai You."

"I think Madame Wu has some theories of her own on that score." Dr. Allen turned to look at Grandma Wu. "Isn't that right?"

"Yes! I've had some time on my hands these last few weeks, so I started doing research on the Song Dynasty. Through my new friend Jiang Fei Fei, the woman in black whom you first saw at the market, I met a retired university historian named Professor Yu who lives here in Feng Jie. He informed us that many of the names you mentioned under hypnosis are well-known historical figures. According to the official Standard History of the Song Dynasty, Cai Jing was indeed Huizong's Prime Minister, and Tong Guan his military commander. The Buddhist Iron Pagoda mentioned by Mei Lan still exists. There were also a few Buddhist nuns of that era who wrote and published poems and lyrics. It's entirely possible that Mei Lan was one of those nuns."

"What about Ah Zhao?" Dr. Allen asked. "Were there Jews living in China so long ago?"

"Absolutely. There's evidence that a few Jewish merchants travelled to Kaifeng 開封, which was formerly called Bian Liang, around that time, to trade cotton goods for silk. The Song Emperor was so pleased with the cloth He received that He allowed the Jews to use His royal surname of Zhao, as well as the surnames of His favorite ministers."

"How sad that Ah Zhao and Zhang Mei Lan didn't end up together!" CC said.

"Oh I don't know . . ." Grandma Wu looked thoughtful. "I like to think that Ah Zhao got away that night and eventually fulfilled his dream of retracing his father's footsteps and discovering his heritage. In any case, he left behind this brilliant painting. By the way, I want to show you something else that's simply amazing!"

Grandma Wu flipped the book over and showed CC a poem printed on the last page. "It says here that this poem was written by a Northern Song Dynasty Buddhist nun named Fo Ni 佛妮. My historian friend, Professor Yu, tells me that Fo Ni was the religious name of Zhang Mei Lan, sister of the famous court painter Zhang Ze Duan. Imagine Mei Lan's poem being published in the same book as the photo of Ah Zhao's painting! How many couples get to have their creative work exhibited together, centuries after their deaths? So, in a way, they have been united after all!"

CC nodded thoughtfully as she turned the pages from the poem to the painting, then back again to the poem.

What we call "death" is really a beginning
"The end" is just another term for being born
Every life is a commencement but also a close
Every epitaph a lullaby

"What a beautiful poem!" CC exclaimed. "It feels so good to look at this painting without that awful feeling of déjà vu that troubled me before. Thank you a million times, Dr. Allen."

Grandma Wu nodded with satisfaction. Then she got up slowly and stretched. "I've been sitting still for far too long. It's time for me to do some *tai chi* 太極 exercises. Now that CC has made a full recovery, Dr. Allen, is it all right for me to take her to Chungking as soon as I can get boat tickets? My son is waiting there for us with our three other young charges: David, Sam and Marat."

Dr. Allen nodded. "We'll miss you both. I hope you'll come back and visit, but I know these are dangerous times. I can't help feeling there will be other difficult journeys ahead for all of us."

Grandma Wu smiled. "It's the journeys we take in our lifetime that make us who we are."

"I hope Big Aunt is happy, wherever she is on her journey," CC said wistfully.

Grandma Wu looked at CC over the top of her glasses. "Don't forget the wonderful poem you just read. 'What we call death is really a beginning.' Your Big Aunt had a great capacity for happiness. I'm sure that remains true, wherever she is now."

"I'm going to copy that poem in my diary," Dr. Allen said. "It will give my terminal patients a lot of comfort to learn it by heart."

"Thank you, Dr. Allen and Grandma Wu," CC said. "I owe a lot to both of you. I'll never forget everything you've done for me."

"No, CC! Trust me! I should be thanking you and

Grandma Wu instead!" Dr. Allen said. "Besides learning a lot of history of the Song Dynasty, I also discovered a whole new way of looking at the world. I used to think there was a logical, scientific explanation for everything—especially medical problems—and that death was something *final:* the absolute end."

CC looked up at him. "So what do you think now?"

Dr. Allen laughed. "In the words of Ah Zhao himself, *you he bu ke?* Is anything impossible?"

How to Pronounce
Chinese Words

Most of the Chinese words and phrases in this book are pronounced as they are written in English. However, here's a short guide on how to say some of the trickier words:

Ba Zi	ba tzer
Cai Jing	chai jing
Cai You	chai yo
cu ju	chew jyu
cun	chun
Da Bi Zi	dah bee zuh
Dong Zhi	dong jer
Gege	guh-guh
Genyue	gun-yue
he li ji qun	huh lee gee chun
Hong Qiao	hong chiao
Huizong	hway-joong
Lei Wei	lay way

Mei Lan	may laan
qi	chee
qin	chin
Qing Ming	ching ming
qing xiao xin	ching shiao shin
Tian Xia Yi Ren	tian shia ee ren
wei qi	way chee
Wu Xing	wu shing
Xiang Long Shi	shiang long shi
Xiao Mei	shiao may
xin	shin
you he bu ke?	yo huh boo kuh?
Ze Duan	zuh duan
Zhang	jaang
Zhao	jow

Glossary of
Chinese Words

Numbers

yi	一	1
er	二	2
san	三	3
si	四	4
wu	五	5
liu	六	6
qi	七	7
ba	八	8
jiu	九	9
shi	十	10

For numbers 11 to 19, join the word for 10 with the unit number, so 11 is *shi yi* 十 一, 12 is *shi er* 十 二 and so on.

Family, Names and People

Ah 阿	a prefix to a name
Ah Li 阿李	the original name of Ah Zhao 阿趙 before Emperor Huizong bestows upon him the royal surname of Zhao
Ah Wang 阿王	Mei Lan's father's number-one manservant
An Kai 安愷	Lady An Kai was the Emperor's favorite concubine, and was the niece of Commissioner Ye Di
baba 爸爸	father
Cai Jing 蔡京	Prime Minister to Emperor Huizong (AD 1047–1126)
Cang Bu Lang Zhong 倉部朗中	Director of the Granary Bureau
Chun Lei 春雷	"Spring Thunder"; name given by Lei Wei to a zither that he made
Confucius 孔子	Chinese philosopher (*c.* 551–547 BC)
Da Bi Zi 大鼻子	"Big Nose"
da ren 大人	magistrate (literally "big person")
Da Si Yue 大司樂	musician-in-chief
Da Yue Ling 大樂令	music officer
dai zhao 待招	imperial attendant
Dian Yue 典樂	music managers
Fo Ni 佛妮	Northern Song Dynasty Buddhist nun, the religious name of Zhang Mei Lan
Gao Bi Zi 高鼻子	"Tall Nose"
gege 哥哥	older brother

Han Lin Hua Yuan Shang Shu 翰林畫院尚書	Director of the Royal Academy of Art
Hu Bu Shang Shu 戶部尚書	Minister of Revenue
Huizong 徽宗	Eighth Emperor of the Song Dynasty (AD 1082–1135; reigned AD 1100–1126)
Jiang Fei Fei 蔣蜚蜚	a friend of CC's Big Aunt
lao ban 老板	proprietor, boss
lao lao 姥姥	maternal grandmother; although Mei Lan would normally only call her birth mother's mother Lao Lao, she uses this term for her stepmother's mother too
Lao Ye 老爺	Old Master (term of address)
Lei Wei 雷威	renowned Tang Dynasty instrument maker, whose name means "Mighty Thunder"
Li Jie 李誡	famous Song Dynasty architect
Lin Ling Su 林靈素	Taoist priest and Huizong's spiritual advisor
Liu Gong Quan 柳公權	Tang Dynasty master of calligraphy (AD 778–865)
Mencius 孟子	Chinese philosopher (*c.* 372–289 BC)
nai ma 奶媽	nanny, wet nurse
nai nai 奶奶	paternal grandmother
niang 娘	mother; also means "young lady"
Shao Ye 少爺	Young Master (term of address)
Tian Xia Yi Ren 天下一人	"First Man of All under Heaven"—cipher of Emperor Huizong
Tian Zi 天子	Son of Heaven
Tong Guan 童貫	military general, court eunuch,

	political advisor to Emperor Huizong (AD 1054–1126)
Wu Nai Nai 吳奶奶	Grandma Wu
Xiao Chen 小陳	Mei Lan's father's coachman; *xiao* 小 (little) is used as a prefix to Chen's name
Xiao Jie 小姐	Little Miss (term of address)
Xie Lu Lang 協律朗	composers
Ye Di 葉棣	commissioner to whom Mei Lan's father is chief assistant
Ye Jia Ming 葉家明	CC's Big Aunt
Ye Xian 葉限	CC's Chinese name
ye ye 爺爺	paternal grandfather
Zhang Mei Lan 張美蘭	Zhang is a family name (surname) and Mei Lan means "Beautiful Orchid"
Zhang Ze Duan 張端	famous court painter (AD 1085–1145)
Zhao 趙	royal surname

Places

Bian Liang 汴梁	capital city of China during the Song Dynasty, located in the eastern Henan province of China; it is now known as Kaifeng 開封
Da Cheng Yue Fu 大晟樂府	Bureau of Music of Great Brilliance
Da Nei 大內	Inner Palace
Da Wai 大外	Outer City
Feng Jie 奉節	a town on the Yangtze River, near the Three Gorges Dam

Genyue 艮嶽	imperial park, commissioned by Emperor Huizong
Han Lin Hua Yuan 翰林畫院	Royal Academy of Art; it was very prestigious to be accepted as a Han Lin scholar
Hong Qiao 虹橋	Rainbow Bridge
Nan Xun Men 南薰門	Southern Infusion Gate
Rui Si Dian 睿思殿	Palace of Divine Inspiration
Tai Hu 太湖	Tai Lake
Tai Miao 太廟	Grand Ancestral Temple
Tie Ta 鐵塔	Iron Pagoda
Wan Qin Lo 萬琴樓	Pavilion of Ten Thousand Zithers
Xuan De Men 宣德門	Gate of Virtue Proclaimed
Yuan Qiu 圓丘	Round Mound Altar

Occasions

Dong Zhi 冬至	Winter Solstice Festival; means "winter has arrived"
Han Shi Jie 寒食節	Cold Food Festival
Li Chun 立春	Spring Equinox
Qing Ming Jie 清明節	Clear and Bright Festival, also called Tomb Sweeping Festival
Xia Zhi 夏至	Summer Solstice
Yuan Xiao Jie 元宵節	Feast of Lanterns

Artistic Works

Da Guan Cha Lun 大觀茶論	*Treatise on Tea;* a classic text by Emperor Huizong on the art of the tea ceremony

189

Lun Yu 論語	*Confucian Analects;* a rulebook for life, made up of discussions Confucius had with his students
Qing Ming Shang He Tu 清明上河圖	*Along the River at Qing Ming* (a painting)
Ting Qin Tu 聽琴圖	*Listening to Zither Music* (a painting)
Xiang Long Shi 祥龍石	*Auspicious Dragon Rock* (a painting)
Zhou Bi Suan Jing 周髀算經	*Astronomy and Mathematics in Ancient China:* one of the oldest classic Chinese texts on mathematics

Sayings

he li ji qun 鶴立雞羣	a crane among hens
tian xia zhi bian yuan 天下之邊緣	at the edge of civilization
you he bu ke? 有何不可?	is anything impossible?

Words and Phrases

Ba Zi 八字	Eight Characters or Eight Words
cao shu 草書	cursive script
chi 尺	a unit of measurement of approximately thirteen inches
cu ju 蹴鞠	football, also called soccer
cun 寸	a unit of measurement of just over one inch
da zi 大字	big characters

190

erhu 二胡	musical instrument like a two-stringed fiddle
fei qian 飛錢	literally "flying money": bank notes made of paper
feng shui 風水	an ancient Chinese system for harmonizing the flow of energy in a room, or building, or other space or structure; literally "wind-water"
feng zheng 風箏	kite
Han Lin 翰林	being a scholar of the Han Lin Academy was very prestigious
Han Ren 漢人	of Han origin
hua 畫	painting
Jin Shi 進士	Imperial Examination, Advanced Scholar Degree
kou-tou 叩頭	to kowtow: to show respect by bowing low and touching one's head to the ground
li 力	strength
li 里	a unit of measurement of approximately one third of a mile
niao 鳥	bird
qi 氣	energy
qin 琴	a zither consisting of a wood frame and seven strings of twisted silk
qing xiao xin 請小心	please be careful
qing, qing 請, 請	please, please
ren 人	man
san bao 三寶	literally "three treasures": three male organs consisting of penis and two testicles
san jue 三絕	three perfections: painting, calligraphy, poetry

sheng xiao 生肖	cycles
shi 詩	poetry
Shi Er Sheng Xiao 十二生肖	Twelve Animals of the Chinese Zodiac: rat, ox, tiger, rabbit, dragon, snake, horse, goat, monkey, rooster, dog and pig
shou jin 瘦金	slender gold calligraphy
shu 書	writing; also means "book"
shu fa 書法	the art of calligraphy
suan pan 算盤	abacus: one of the earliest devices for counting and doing calculations
tai chi 太極	a Chinese martial art practiced to promote good health
Tian 天	Heaven
Tian Wen 天文	Language of Heaven (the study of astronomy)
Tian Xia 天下	Land under Heaven
tong bi 銅幣	copper coins
tu zhang 圖章	chop, stamp, seal or symbol
wai ren 外人	an outsider; someone who doesn't belong
wei qi 圍棋	go, a game of strategy for two players, played with "stones" on a board covered with gridlines; the aim is to control as much of the board as possible
wen fang si bao 文房四寶	Four Treasures of the Scholar: ink-stick 墨 (*mo*), ink-stone 硯 (*yan*), brush 筆 (*bi*) and paper 紙 (*zhi*)
Wu Xing 五行	Five Elements
xin 心	heart

Ya Yue 雅樂	Proper Music
yamen 衙門	government office
Yin – Yang 陰－陽	essential 'forces' or underlying principles in life that are opposites yet balanced, separate yet interdependent
Yin Yue 淫樂	Improper and Licentious Music
zhang 丈	a unit of measurement of almost eleven feet; ten *chi* make one *zhang*

Author's Note

This book is a fantasy based on the ancient Chinese painting titled *Along the River at Qing Ming*. Nicknamed China's *Mona Lisa* by Chinese-art lovers because of its fame, it was painted in the twelfth century by a court artist named Zhang Ze Duan. During the subsequent dynasties, it has been in the private collection of many Chinese emperors. More than twenty copies were made by various artists.

Pu Yi, the last Emperor of the Qing Dynasty, abdicated his throne in 1912. Nevertheless, he lived in the Forbidden Palace until 1924. When he finally left under duress, he took *Along the River at Qing Ming* with him. In 1932, he went to Manchuria and was installed by the Japanese as the puppet Emperor of Manchukuo (Manchuria) in 1934.

In 1945, the Japanese lost the Second World War and Pu Yi fled from Manchuria. He was captured by the Russians, who put him in jail and placed his painting in a vault at the Bank of China.

In 1950, the Russians returned Pu Yi to Communist China for trial as a war criminal. Meanwhile, his painting was transferred to the Palace Museum in Beijing, where it remains to this day. Mao Ze-dong pardoned Pu Yi in 1959. He worked as a gardener in the Beijing Botanical Gardens after his release from prison, and died eight years later during the Cultural Revolution.

This book is based on the fictional character CC (initials for Chinese Cinderella). CC must leave the boat used in an espionage mission to buy food in the river town of Feng Jie. Pursued by a strange woman dressed in black, she escapes by climbing up a drainpipe but then falls from the roof. She is taken to a hospital. On awakening from a coma, CC is treated for her neurological symptoms. While under hypnosis, she recalls the life she led eight hundred years ago as a young girl in Bian Liang (now called Kaifeng), the capital of China during the Northern Song Dynasty.

Two other paintings are mentioned in this book: *Auspicious Dragon Rock* and *Listening to Zither Music*, both also housed at the Palace Museum in Beijing. They are attributed to Emperor Huizong, whose signature, written in cipher (First Man of All under Heaven—*Tian Xia Yi Ren* 天 下 一 人), and seal mark can be seen to the left of the two paintings.

My research was carried out at the library of the University of California, Irvine. Although CC, Zhang Mei Lan and Ah Zhao are all fictional characters, the paintings are real. So are the supporting cast of individuals—such as Tong Guan, the eunuch general, and Cai Jing, the Prime Minister—as well as the book's historical background.

The following two books were enormously helpful: *Emperor Huizong and Late Northern Song China* by Patricia Ebrey and Maggie Bickford and *Palace Women in the Northern Sung* by Priscilla Ching Chung.

About the Author

Adeline Yen Mah was born in Tianjin, China, and trained to be a doctor in London. She has had a distinguished career in medicine in the United States for many years. Her memoir for adults, *Falling Leaves*, was a worldwide bestseller and was translated into eighteen languages. *Chinese Cinderella* is her memoir for young adults. Adeline divides her time between Los Angeles, London, Shanghai, and Hong Kong. Visit her at AdelineYenMah.com.